Behind the Lies

A NOVEL

MAREN COOPER

SHE WRITES PRESS

Published 2023
Printed in the United States of America
Print ISBN: 978-1-64742-587-6
E-ISBN: 978-1-64742-588-3
Library of Congress Control Number: 2023909284

For information, address:
She Writes Press
1569 Solano Ave #546
Berkeley, CA 94707

Interior Design by Tabitha Lahr

She Writes Press is a division of SparkPoint Studio, LLC.

"The saddest thing about betrayal is that it never comes from your enemies, it comes from those you trust the most."

—ANONYMOUS

CHAPTER 1

The cryptic message from Chet pulled Will out of the office in the middle of a workday, no questions asked. Chet was probably the only person who could get away with that these days, but he had a power over Will no one else did. And it wasn't just because Chet Sutherland was a legend in biotech circles or because he'd been grooming Will to be BioteKem's next CEO. It was because he'd become a father figure and source of life wisdom for Will.

Will punched the unknown address from Chet's text into his GPS and drove, wondering where exactly he was going. When he crossed into the Mystic Lakes area, he remembered Chet's stories about family fun at the boat club in Medford, when he and his first wife had lived there. But Chet and his second wife, Andrea, lived in Waltham now. Plus, early March in Massachusetts wasn't the best time to enjoy a boat club.

As Will drove up and saw the harsh treatment the season had served up, he hoped it wasn't membership recruitment time. He took off his cashmere overcoat and folded it on the passenger seat with his gloves, leaving his sunglasses on for the quick dash into the club. He took a quick look in the mirror as he palmed his cheeks, wondering if he would have time to shave before the night's activities. He was glad for the recent haircut; his dark, curly hair looked best when well-tended. He smiled at himself and locked the car.

The lake was mostly iced over, and the wind whipped his scarf as he walked carefully on the packed snow and ice, which covered most of the walkways. With his hands in his pockets, he followed a shoveled path past the dry-rack boat storage toward an almost deserted clubhouse, which badly needed some fresh paint. The back of the building toward the water glistened. The late winter sun was still strong enough to cast reflective light off the glass and steel of the conservatory, which appeared to be a recent add-on. With nobody at the entrance, he made his way by following the light. The glint caused Will to squint as he headed to the far corner of the conservatory to find Chet, his body in outline, the only person in the cavernous space. When Will reached Chet's table, he said, "Talk about meeting off the beaten track. This has got to be the loneliest corner of the city. What's up?"

Only then did he notice his boss's face as he turned his phone over and set it on the table. Beads of perspiration lined Chet's forehead, threatening to rain down on his graying temples. His red face was marred by blotches of white, one corner of his shirt collar askew. But it was Chet's narrowed, gray-blue eyes that announced the real sea change in his feelings toward Will.

"Sit."

"Chet, are you all right? You don't look so good. Can I get you some water or something else?" His eyes landed on the glass on the table. Bourbon? Will searched the empty room, hoping for a waiter or any other interruption to change the mood of the encounter.

"I'm not all right, no. I've been betrayed. By someone who I trusted. Someone who I mentored. Someone who I thought I knew. Whose values I thought were similar to mine." His voice trailed off as he took the last of his drink. "Someone I thought was superior to me in intelligence . . ." He scoffed. "What a fool I've been."

"Chet, what are you talking about. What's got you so upset?" Will's mind raced. He had never seen Chet so rattled. The man had a well-deserved reputation for staying unruffled through tense negotiations to the annoyance of business adversaries trying to throw him off his game. It was like playing chess with a grand master—pointless to find a weak spot because it didn't exist.

Will thought back to their last meeting. Routine. Just updates on the various ventures BioteKem had initiated. Running a twelve-billion-dollar global biotech company always had its challenges, but nothing of late was causing too much heartburn. In truth, Chet had dialed back the frequency of these meetings. Will, current president and COO, was poised to take over as board chair and CEO within the calendar year. Chet was nearing sixty-six and eager to enjoy a retirement adventure or two. They were just waiting for the right time to announce the change to avoid any undue upset in the stock price. Little more than a figurehead now, he spent any company time golfing with VIPs and chairing the quarterly meetings.

Will chided himself as he recalled his first thought when the request for this impromptu meeting came in this morning. *Chet wants to discuss the timing. Maybe he feels ready? Or he wants to up my bonus for the spectacular results for the last calendar year, just in.*

"You can't guess? Then you aren't as smart as I thought you were." Chet slurred his words.

Will stared at Chet, hoping to find the man he knew and not this tipsy imposter wearing Chet's clothes.

"Chet, can I drive you home? Is Andrea meeting you at the hotel?" Will thought about the evening gala coming up in just a few hours. Both men were expected to be there as BioteKem was to win an award at the Annual Global Healthcare Summit event. Chet needed to sober up.

"Don't concern yourself with me now, Will. It's much too late." He scoffed and checked his watch. "I have a car coming in five minutes. Just enough time for me to tell you your time is up."

"What are you talking about?"

"I'm calling an emergency board meeting for next week. With one agenda item—your dismissal. I'm firing you, Will." Chet's eyes, cold as ice, held Will's for a moment. Then he used the arms of the chair to steady himself as he rose.

Will stared at him, openmouthed. Finally, he stammered, "What? Why?"

"Chasing tail is adolescent, Will. And chasing tail when offered for a business trade is fatal. When the product is a fraud, stupid and unforgivable."

Chet fumbled to pocket his phone, straightened his back, and moved smoothly across the room, as if from a chess match with an inferior player.

CHAPTER 2

W ill stood to follow, then stopped and quickly sat down. His legs suddenly weak, he wasn't sure he could trust muscle memory to move his body with his brain in a frenzy. How could he be fired? Then he remembered Chet's comment. *Chasing tail.* His body froze at the thought that Chet knew about his fling. But he couldn't know. Will had been careful. Never meeting in public other than at a large business lunch or event. Hotel assignations not under his name. It was a novel game for him. He couldn't resist the flattery of her pursuit of him, the frisson of a new woman something he never considered as a potential temptation.

So crass to think of it as "chasing tail." He would never have expected to hear those words coming from Chet. His face flushed in shame as he admitted to himself the description fit, but he shook it off. What he needed to focus on now was finding out what was going on with Chet. He tightened his fists to gain control and rolled his shoulders slowly.

A waiter approached apologetically. "I'm so sorry, I didn't see another person arrive. Can I bring you something?"

"No. Thanks. I'll be leaving myself." Will watched him take the empty glass and realized it had only been a ten-minute meeting. Had it even really happened? He couldn't move. Firing people was his realm, not being fired himself. It was a cost of doing business, however unpleasant. He had strategized about how to fire many people over the years, some for the right reasons, and some . . . well, it's what happened when you had a global enterprise to run. But this could never happen to him.

He took a deep breath and as he exhaled, an involuntary chuckle escaped. He shook his head. Who was that man pretending to be Chet? Where was the Chet who described Will as the honorary son who came along at the right time and gave him an opening to confidently leave BioteKem? That Will was the only one Chet could trust to keep it solid, for the good of the patients who depended on their products and kept the stockholders happy enough to continue the R&D necessary to stay on mission.

Maybe Chet was sick. He didn't look good. Maybe he was paranoid, having a psychotic break.

His phone buzzed. A text from his wife.

Yes, I sent your tux to the office. Good luck tonight.

The message pulled him from his stupor. Charlotte was responding to a text he had sent this morning when he remembered he needed his tux for the event and wouldn't be going home beforehand. He had made plans to meet up with Bella for the night. They would each attend the dinner, separately, but Bella, a budding star in the biotech world, would leave her hotel room empty and join him for the night and a leisurely morning together. This time, he promised himself, he would actually start the process of mentoring her.

He parked any further worries about Chet along with his car in his personal parking space and headed into his office in Kendall Square.

BioteKem's headquarters in North America was perfectly situated in the midst of Boston's biotechnology community. Its solid, ten-story building rose like a beacon among its neighbors, befitting its position as one of the pioneers who kept getting stronger, and set the pace for the newer companies in class and innovation.

Since Will's arrival twenty-four months ago, he knew he was moving it faster now, proud of his track record. It had taken focus, but compartmentalizing life was his forte. His home life was the easiest, handing it over to Charlotte. While it had not been discussed explicitly, he knew she had expected to be in charge of their family life. She had envisioned and forged the path for his transformation from his somewhat geeky academic persona into a successful entrepreneur businessman, forfeiting her career aspirations in Public Relations along the way. Her natural curiosity and knowledge of the medical field and its star researchers eventually led her to a more meaningful side gig. She helped patients with rare diseases find clinical trials that might help them. It was rewarding as well as flexible for child-rearing and their lifestyle as they moved around the world for his career. He traveled extensively but enjoyed the role of Dad who showed up for events, provided for the expensive tastes in houses, activities, and vacations, and occasionally paraded them at his company events to show off the perfect family.

He stayed connected to academic life by providing internships at BioteKem for the bright lights at the best colleges, keeping an adjunct faculty appointment alive at Penn. He ensured his PR team stayed active in soliciting invitations for his participation in the right panels and roundtable discussions at industry-wide meetings. Branded as the scientist who made it big in biotech, he was always sought after. He could still speak the academic language, but it didn't thrill him anymore. The young man who searched for cures and treatments for neurological and circulatory diseases for the sake of humankind was gone; he had happily sold out for higher rewards and to make a bigger contribution on the global stage.

What did motivate him was making deals. He had a few in the works, and the thrill of discovery of how to make a deal replaced his former passion to search for success in the lab. Increasingly, he followed his own business instincts and brought Chet in later in the process, confident Chet would not second-guess him but merely admire his handiwork to celebrate the success together.

The office was quiet when he got there. His executive assistant, Merilee, had his tux hanging on the door to his office closet. She had turned down the lights and had lamplight on for him as dusk was close. He liked watching the lights of the city go on as he swiveled in his desk chair and looked out at the panoramic view of the Charles River. He read email curated by Merilee and considered whether he should change into his tux now or take it with him to change at the hotel. He smiled thinking about the festive nature of fancy dress and taking it off and kept his tux on the hanger.

He took an Uber to the Intercontinental Boston Hotel and approached reception, credit card in hand. "Will Franklin."

The young hotel clerk smiled warmly. "Good evening, Dr. Franklin." She turned to the computer screen. "I see your wife has already checked in."

"No, Mrs. Franklin isn't coming, just me tonight." It wasn't uncommon for Charlotte to skip these events, although she did like the glitz of dressing up sometimes. But this weekend their son Andy had a swim meet that interfered with a night in town for her. She had declined.

"Umm, I do have a Mrs. Franklin checked in about thirty minutes ago. Could you be mistaken, sir?" The young woman was flustered and picked up the phone to call the room.

Will pondered, then quickly stopped her. "No, don't bother. I could be mistaken." He considered the possibility that Bella had posed as his wife and checked into his room. He was instantly furious at the audacity of it. How could she dare? How would he manage to keep the pretense of distance if she was in his room this early? Alongside his fury, the steady beat of desire gained traction, leaving any remaining thoughts of Chet behind him.

Merilee always reserved him a suite on an upper floor. He had Bella's room number. She could take the stairs up a few floors and nobody would be the wiser. At least, that was the plan. He was nearly panting by the time he used his key card to open the door. Low light and music in the sitting room greeted him, with a bottle of wine chilling. He put his overnight bag down and hung his tux on the back of a chair.

"Hello?"

He walked into the bedroom and heard water running in the adjoining bath. His peripheral vision picked up a slinky black dress on a door hook. He was about to study the dress more closely to pick up a clue when the water stopped and a woman wrapping herself in a towel stepped into the bedroom.

"Ohh hi, handsome. How do you like my surprise?"

Stunned for the second time that afternoon, Will stared at her and finally spoke. "Charlotte."

"Wow, I guess it worked. You look totally shocked." She dropped the towel and still dripping wet, walked naked across the floor to him and raised herself to her tiptoes to give him a big kiss, without touching any other part of his body. "I thought we needed a special night. It's been too long." She grabbed the hotel robe from the closet. "So, when you texted me this morning about the tux, I pictured you going to this dull event and sitting through it on your own." She frowned. "So, I got on the phone to make arrangements for Andy to go to the meet with Chaz and his mom, and voila, here I am!" She laughed. "I thought I was really clever to send you that text later about sending your tux to the office. I wanted to keep the surprise under wraps. How did I do?" She flopped onto the bed.

Will recovered enough to respond. "Wow, you did great," as his mind raced through various scenarios of this evening that could keep him intact. For a full minute, he wished he was the man who could appreciate the expression of love from his wife that led her here and unwrap her robe to show her how much. But he had chosen not to live a simple life.

He needed to get to Bella before disaster struck. "So glad you came. You'll make all the difference in the evening." He gave her a quick peck on the cheek and rushed on. "Let me wash up and we can have a glass of wine before we go down to the event. I see you have some chilling. Very good move on your part." He blew her a last kiss and excused himself to the bathroom.

CHAPTER 3

Will closed the bathroom door and looked up at the ceiling, breathing deeply. *What a mess!* He hated to text Bella but had no choice.

Tonight won't work. Sorry.

After clicking off, he realized he sounded like a jerk. But he didn't want to go into details, and any explanation at this point would be lame. He'd make it up to her later.

Charlotte was luminous in the black dress. She was finishing her makeup and jewelry when he returned. He had always loved watching her get ready. A natural beauty, she seemed to be ageless. Even in her mid-forties, she remained the center of attention in any room she entered. She smiled at him.

"Zip me up?"

He kissed her bare shoulder. "You look gorgeous."

She studied his face. "Are you all right? You seem uptight. Is there something going on that I should know about?"

He put on his best blank look. "Nope, all is good."

Her intuition was uncanny. Even though he hadn't been sharing everything as in their earlier years, she could usually figure him out. He had been putting distance between them, and the intimacy of those days was gone. The years when she was in his head, guiding his career moves, were over. Then, he had been grateful for her instincts and guidance, but now, clearly aware of his own power, he had outgrown the habit. He hadn't left her behind so much as freed her from feeling obligated to stay current with his business maneuvers.

It was Charlotte taking charge of their relocations that left her little time to keep up with every business deal he was involved in. Moving them seamlessly, with two children in tow, was no easy feat. Navigating the cultural changes in moves to Europe and Asia was challenging as well, but she seemed to relish leading the way. They didn't discuss it, but she also seemed to appreciate the opportunity to explore new interests on her own.

In Barcelona, he remembered when she asked him whether he minded if she committed to assist the chef in teaching tourists in an immersive Catalan cooking course. She had searched his face for approval.

"It may interrupt our usual routine. I won't be as available. Is that okay?"

An unspoken telepathy passed between them. Will registered a request from his wife to find something just for herself, and he was more than ready for her to do so. He loved what he was doing, and she had helped get him there. But he was good to go it alone moving forward.

"Of course, you should do it!" They had sealed the unspoken new pact with a sweet kiss. Now, his lovely bride had surprised him again.

"Well," she said, "I know I haven't been very accessible of late; not taking care of my man the way I like to. I promise I'll be paying more attention." She put both hands on his cheeks and gave him a quick kiss, then playfully pushed him away. "You have time to shave. Go take your shower, and you can get gorgeous in your tux, too. Then we can toast our night out, make whatever appearance we need to make at the event, and sneak out . . . for our own personal party." She winked at him.

———————✦———————

The hotel ballroom was festooned with garlands of silvery snowflakes. Purple and tangerine lanterns were fitted with twinkling lights. A side room for the VIP reception was already crowded by the time Charlotte and Will arrived. A string quartet played in a corner. The Annual Global Healthcare Summit, sponsored by the world's largest pharmaceutical companies, was a must event for networking over substance, and the awards program itself was fairly superficial. BioteKem had won the grand prize last year and wasn't up for anything big this year. But it was not an event he could miss.

Will was swarmed as soon as they entered the room. With Charlotte on his arm, he was excused from too much shop talk, and fortunately, the conversation with the European reps was mostly about the weather, the puzzle of American politics, and the economic outlook in Europe after Brexit.

The dinner bell announced the ballroom opening, and Will led Charlotte to their assigned table. As they wound their way through the crowded space to the front of the room, Charlotte nudged him. "Isn't that Andrea and Chet? Looks like they're going the wrong way."

Before he could stop his wife, she was on her way to them, and he was in a conversation with a tablemate. She rejoined him quickly and introductions were made all around. Privately he asked her, "So, did you catch them?"

"Yes, they were leaving. Andrea just gave me a quick hug and told me Chet wasn't feeling well. He didn't even say hello to me. Do you know what's going on with him?"

"No, sorry to hear that. Hope he's okay. That was all?" Will passed the rolls.

When she confirmed nothing else was said, he relaxed a bit. While he hadn't put Chet's words totally out of his mind, his mysterious disappearance bolstered the theory Chet was not himself. He was more preoccupied with where Bella might be. He hadn't expected her to attend the reception but thought he might see her at the dinner. Her goal in attending was to meet with prospective angel investors for her new company, and he assumed she would be trying to network heavily. He stood up a couple of times to scan the room with no luck.

Charlotte was playing footsie with him, and it was working. He noted how several of the men at the table seemed to bring her into every conversation. One of them, a researcher who recognized her name as the woman who helped a desperately ill patient connect with his clinical trial took the time to praise her for her work. She blushed and acknowledged the satisfaction she felt when making a match and how stories like this were so appreciated.

She thanked him and then led the table talk away from business by asking, "What is your most favorite thing to do or eat in America when you come here?" which kept the group amused.

When one visitor from France confessed to a fondness for Kentucky Fried Chicken, she proudly announced, "And you sir, are a connoisseur of the highest order. The closest one is just a quick Uber ride away!"

He was beginning to think an early escape and a night of lovemaking with his wife would end this trying day, but when she asked if they could go to the after-party for a drink before going up, he couldn't refuse. When she pulled him to the dance floor and nibbled on his ear, he was in thrall to his wife of seventeen years.

He whispered, "Let's go upstairs and make love," and she melted into his arms.

As he led her from the dance floor, he saw Bella, sitting at the bar, staring at him. Their eyes met. His first reflex was to drop Charlotte's hand. Then, he regained his wits and stared back at her, dropping his eyes quickly as he registered the raw anger . . . or hurt?

He would have to deal with her tomorrow.

Much later, Will was awakened by a text. He slid from the bed and picked up his phone. His body sated by the healing love of his wife, he covered her body gently, tousled blond hair trailing down her back. He shook off any remaining buzz from the alcohol and quietly went to the sitting room. Not many people would text him in the middle of the night, and very few had this number. Merilee screened most on a different line. Then he remembered Bella and her anger.

But it was Andrea.

Chet fell in the bathroom and is having trouble talking to me.

Where should I have the ambulance take him? Call me.

Chet! He was sick! He knew something was wrong. He clicked in her number, then scrolled through his contacts as he waited for her to answer.

"Andrea, it's me. Where are you?'

"Will, thank God." He heard the catch in her throat. "Still in our room, but the emergency techs are coming up from the lobby. What should I do?"

"Okay, they'll quickly assess. If they tell you they need to take him to their nearest emergency hospital, I don't think you should argue the point. They know which hospital is best able to accept a patient with Chet's issues. But if they ask you where to take him, tell them Mass General. I'm going to make a call to a contact there now, so they'll be ready. Okay?"

"Yes, thanks Will."

"Can you describe what's going on with Chet?"

"We assumed he was coming down with the flu and decided on an early night, but his headache just kept getting worse. Then, nausea got him to the bathroom, and I heard him fall. I think he may have hit his head. Will, I'm scared."

"It's okay, Andrea, I'm here." He considered how long it would take him to pull on his pants and go to her. "Listen, text me when you know where they're taking him, and I'll meet you there." Will heard a commotion as the EMTs arrived.

"Gotta go." She hung up abruptly.

He wasn't sure if she had heard his request. 3:05 a.m. Fully awake now, he paced until he received another text from Andrea.

Mass General.

With that, he clicked his friend Clark's number and grabbed his pants. "You've reached Dr. Clark Boyd's voice mail. I'm not on service right now. If this is a medical emergency, please hang up and call 911. If you have a nonemergent issue, please call my office. If you—"

"Damn." He scribbled a quick note to Charlotte, finished dressing, and was out the door and in the lobby in five minutes. By then, he had texted Merilee to find Clark Boyd's home phone number and have him call ASAP.

Massachusetts General Hospital, not too far away, was the original and largest teaching hospital of Harvard Medical

School located in the West End neighborhood of Boston. Clark Boyd was a research scientist he had known for years. Recently BioteKem had selected his lab for clinical trials with great results. He was also a gifted internist, who had an active practice and supervised residents on service at the hospital.

By the time Will arrived at the hospital, Clark had called him and agreed to make contact with the emergency room to inquire about Chet's condition.

Andrea jumped when he approached her in the waiting room. "Oh, it's you. Thank God." She reached out to take his outstretched hand, and her eyes immediately filled with tears.

He took her hand. "Andrea, I'm here. We'll sort this out." He noticed she had spent even less time dressing than he had. He could see her nightgown peeking from her trench coat, which she kept belted and wore with a pair of black, patent dress shoes. Her red hair was pulled back into a tie, her face a white mask of fear without makeup.

"What's happening now?"

"I'm not sure. The EMTs put him on oxygen right away and asked me lots of questions. "Could he have hit his head when he fell? Had he been exposed to any toxic chemicals? Was he allergic to anything that he may have eaten? When did his headache start? When we got here, they whisked him away and I haven't seen him since."

"Was he able to talk to them at all?"

"No, he's kind of out of it. Almost like he's out of reach." She squeezed his hand. "Even earlier last evening, he was not talkative. Like he was upset and mulling over something."

"He didn't tell you about anything that was bothering him?" He held his breath. He was prepared to mention Chet's odd behavior earlier yesterday afternoon, but only if it fit the narrative she had been relaying.

"No. You know him." She smiled. "He keeps things pretty close to the vest. At least with me, that is. I know he confides in you. He trusts you implicitly. Thanks for helping me out tonight. I didn't know who else . . ."

"Happy to help. You did the right thing to reach out. We'll take care of it."

He liked Andrea. Chet's second wife was closer in age to him and Charlotte than to Chet. She was somewhat intimidated by her husband, but Chet doted on her and their son, Danny. His first marriage had not been a happy one. When his wife had died, he tried too late to deepen a relationship with his teenaged daughter, but she was bitter about the years of fatherly neglect, and Chet realized then how important it was to be an active parent and spouse.

Around 6:00 a.m., Clark called him before they had any word from the emergency room. He stepped away from Andrea to take the call.

"Your friend is not in very good shape. They've done the scans and run the lab work they needed. They're trying to determine whether he could have suffered a traumatic brain injury when he fell in the bathroom. But right now, it looks like he may have had a massive stroke. They need to admit him right away and treat him aggressively.

"You're kidding. Really? Chet hasn't had any major health issues that I'm aware of."

"I don't know about his health history, just what I was told he presented with, and it's a serious hemorrhage. As far as we've come with treatments for neurological issues, sometimes you just can't prepare for the big one; and unfortunately, that could be what's going on with your friend."

"No, that can't be." His raised voice caught Andrea's attention, and she approached him, mouthing, *What?*

Clark promised to stay on it, and Will thanked him. He wasn't sure how to tell Andrea. Fortunately, an emergency room physician called her name, and he didn't have to.

CHAPTER 4

Will moved away to give Andrea some privacy with the doctor, but after she collapsed in the nearest chair with the doctor's news, she beckoned him over.

"Will, please help me take in what's going on. The doctor is telling me Chet is not conscious."

Will quickly introduced himself as a family friend there to help and the young physician gratefully repeated his dire news, exactly what Will had already learned from Clark.

"How sure are you that it's a stroke and not a TBI? And what does that mean?"

"We've reviewed the scans and the lab work. It's looking like Mr. Sutherland has suffered a stroke."

"What happens next?" Will asked.

"At this point, it's a waiting game. I recommend Mrs. Sutherland go home and get some rest and stay in touch with us. We'll be admitting him to the ICU shortly, and we're close to making the call to place him on a ventilator to keep his lungs functioning."

"I understand. Thank you, Doctor." Will nodded at him and turned his attention to Andrea as the doctor left them.

"This can't be happening." Andrea started to hyperventilate. Will pulled her from the chair and walked with her a bit, his arm around her shoulder, reassuring her this was the best place for Chet. It took some time to convince her she should leave, but finally she agreed to let him take her back to the hotel.

He knew she was exhausted because he was. His immediate goal was to keep her going until she could get home and safely away from the hospital. "Where's Danny right now?"

Andrea bolted upright in the car. "Oh my God. Danny. What time is it? Where's my phone?"

"It's still early. Just after seven." He inspected Andrea, who hadn't even brought a purse with her. "Could your phone be in your coat pocket?"

She pulled it out and checked text messages, exhaling loudly. "Good. The last message was the one I sent you. Danny hasn't called for a ride home yet. He's staying with a friend." She gave him a quick smile of relief. "But I need to get home before he does."

"Yes, that would be good for both of you." He smiled at her, his mind moving fast on any other immediate actions to take. "Do you have a car at the hotel, and if you do, do you feel like you are up to driving? It's been quite a shock, and I know you must be exhausted."

"Thanks for looking out for me." She patted his hand. "But I'm getting my second wind now thinking about Danny. I'll quickly pack up and drive home."

An hour later, Will had showered and was making himself a cup of coffee from the self-serve in the room when there was a light knock on the door. From a corner of his brain, an image of Bella came to him, and he remembered that they were to spend the morning together with a late checkout, in his room. He used the peephole and sighed with relief. He opened the door to Andrea, dressed and ready to go home.

"Will, I can't ever thank you enough for your help. I'm hoping you are still willing." Her voice was strong but tentative. She smiled, and he noticed a bit of color had come back to her face.

"Whatever you need, I'll help you through this. What is it?"

"This feels a little weird, but I've got Chet's phone and laptop, and I assume there will be some business that needs to be attended to. I was hoping you could take that on for us?"

Will's heart jumped. He looked at the case in her outstretched arm and swallowed. Andrea wanted him to take over Chet's communications. He understood the request to keep the continuity secured, but to hand it over to him totally? Clearly, she had no hint of a potential change of status between the men. As time moved forward, he wasn't sure it had even happened. Without hesitation, Will accepted it for the gift horse or supportive duty it was.

"Of course, Andrea. I'll do it."

She handed him a small case with both devices and hurriedly gave him a hug. "Thanks, Will."

"Was that a woman's voice I heard?" Charlotte's teasing voice reached him from the bedroom. "Are you entertaining other lovers while I sleep in?"

Will blanched, avoiding her eyes. As usual, his wife had nailed it. He was supposed to be entertaining a lover in this very suite at this precise time. He was still unsure how he had succumbed to Bella's charms. Then an unbidden image of her lovely body flooded his senses, reminding him of his weakness. Charlotte walked toward him lazily, belting her robe, but stopped when she saw his face. "What is it? What do you have there?"

Will put the case on the table next to the note he had left her, obviously unread, and pulled her to sit with him on the couch. He needed a minute. The events of the last two days were catching up with him. Her softness and warmth so stark against the reality of Chet's compromised mortality brought out a vulnerability that surprised him.

"It's bad, Charlotte," he whispered. He told her what had happened, his voice wobbly with fatigue and disbelief.

She listened attentively, encouraging him to give her all of the details.

"Poor Andrea," Charlotte, teary-eyed, said when Will had finished.

A knock on the door surprised them both.

"Room Service."

"Did you think to order breakfast?" Charlotte asked him, heading to answer the door.

Will remembered the plans he had made to have a luxurious breakfast with Bella after their night together. He saved himself and said, "Yes, I ordered when I got back from the hospital. I thought we could have a bite together here before I head back to the office."

"Wow, what a feast!" She eyed the full breakfast for two with pastries, smoked salmon, and bagels. "That was smart. Given the day ahead of you, this may be the only meal you get, and I can take some of it home with me. Surprised you ordered smoked salmon. I know that must have been for me. Thanks."

She poured herself some coffee and picked up the *New York Times* from the cart. "Oh God!" She held it up for him to see.

"ENGER PHARMACEUTICALS HACKED While International Leaders Convene at the Annual Global Healthcare Summit," the headline read, and just below that, *"Industry-Wide Effort to Determine Scale of Attack."*

Will walked Charlotte to the valet to get her car, and then to his Uber to go to the office. He and Merilee had been texting back and forth for the past hour. He had directed her to prepare an internal announcement about Chet for just the top tier of management and a possible press release, if needed. Yes, Chet Sutherland was in the hospital, no more details as of yet.

Just an hour ago, his primary task was to get into Chet's phone and laptop. Now the cyberattack of unknown dimension held his primary focus. But Merilee had contacted IT to send someone to his office to unlock the computer. Andrea had left a Post-it note of the phone's passcode in the case for him. He told himself Andrea wanted him to take care of business and that Chet would have wanted him to do so. Still, he felt like a sneak. His core survival instinct was to find out if there was anything on the computer that would explain the accusations Chet had leveled at him yesterday. Specifically, he wanted to know if there were any plans for an emergency board meeting in the next week.

BioteKem security was light on Saturday, and Will greeted the weekend guard and headed up to his corner office on the 10th floor. The IT guy waited for him outside the executive suite, and Will wasted no time with small talk.

"Get me in ASAP." He had just opened Chet's iPhone when he saw Nick Offerman, Chief of European Operations, through the glass.

Nick, dressed in work-out gear and a hoodie, his earbuds dangling, seemed ready to blast off when he burst through Will's door and announced, "We've got problems in Italy. There's been a security breach at the Lombardy plant. Don't know if it's related to the hack. The production line is down. They want permission to shut down."

Will calmly stowed Chet's iPhone in his desk drawer and said, "Okay, we're gonna have a full-blown emergency situation worldwide. This is the beginning. Let's get everybody in. I'll have Merilee get the emergency command group here now." He started a text.

Will's body relaxed. Exhilaration replaced the fatigue he should have felt. He was in his zone. Focusing on command leadership with a crisis brewing was his sweet spot. He didn't get nervous, he got smart. And his team responded.

"You look frazzled, Nick, did you get a good run in?" Will grinned. "May be your last one for a day or two." He swiveled his chair away from his desk and took Nick's elbow and steered him to the hallway. "Let's get the conference room set up for our command center. There's an IT guy here now. We can have him get a few more monitors ready."

Ten hours later, the command center still hummed. Global operations were reporting into the group of seven execs situated in the conference room in all manner of casual attire and posture. Some sat upright in a chair, others used a chair for their feet. Pizza boxes from hours before were piled atop the credenza alongside the window with used paper plates scattered around the table. Big Pharma was closing down what they could for twenty-four hours. The cybersecurity chiefs across the biotech industry had established a war room and were into the discovery phase of scanning to see how widespread the hack was.

Will and his team mined their formal and informal networks to get information from the trade associations and start a dialogue with the FBI. Someone had contacted the National Security Agency. All information was reported into the entire group to have redundancy of intelligence.

Scarlett, the UK expert, was the first to ask the obvious question. "So, are we going to break sometime soon? I either need to eat again or go home."

Will looked around the room at his weary team and laughed. "My God, this looks like a college cram session." He beamed. "We've made a good start. I think we'll perform better after we get some sleep." Noting the collective sigh of relief, he added. "Good work today. Remember, with what looks like a widespread threat, our patients still need to get their meds, and with any luck, after our strategy session today, and more to come, we have a shot at minimizing the damage to the supply chain. There will be enough pain in the world without adding to it."

As the group scattered, Will realized he hadn't checked with Andrea since that morning and had missed a text from Clark.

No good news on Chet.

He hoped it wasn't too late to call her, but she picked up after the second ring. She had been back to the hospital. Danny was okay, and she was just going to bed.

"He didn't even acknowledge me. I'm really worried." Her voice broke. "I don't know what I can do for him."

"I think you're doing it. Taking care of yourself and Danny is what he would want you to be doing. Try to get some rest. I'll check in with you again tomorrow."

Only then did he remember Chet's devices locked up in his desk. He considered taking them home but decided against it. He needed a night with his own family to face tomorrow, and whatever he found out then.

CHAPTER 5

Leaving the office in Kendall Square at this hour on a Saturday made his drive to Belmont much faster, although snow flurries were starting. As he turned into his circle drive, the snow falling against the brick facade of the house well-lit with ground and entry lights made for a lovely New England winter scene. Hope flitted through his mind that the pure white flakes could cover over the events of the weekend as easy as they would cover over the gray slush from the previous week's attempt at a thaw.

Will had texted Charlotte and told her not to wait up. The house was still. He walked through the expanse of the open-design first floor and looked out at the deck and patio to the backyard tennis court. He considered making himself a drink but didn't want to dull his thoughts. Today's work had reminded him of the steady adrenaline rush of his early days in the lab when concentration was total, and teamwork was what kept one going. He called upon that memory to let his body start to shut down any lingering worries.

He climbed the stairs and peeked into Andy's room. His pulse slowed when he saw his ten-year-old peacefully asleep with his stuffed toys pushed to the side but not off of the bed. His latest LEGO project in progress was placed on a nearby table.

"Ahhh. Ouch!" Will exclaimed quietly after his foot caught a LEGO, as he gingerly navigated the space over to his son's bed and pulled the blanket up.

After dropping his clothes to the floor in his walk-in closet, he put on pajamas and slipped into bed beside Charlotte. She sighed without waking totally and turned her body into his, repositioning his arm to allow for her head to rest on his chest and scissoring her leg over his. He fell asleep before he had to consider whether he deserved his loving wife and family. The close call of the weekend's misadventure with Bella was running a close second to his worries about Chet. The ultimate threat—the possibility of Charlotte finding out about Bella—loomed too large to take on right now.

———————❖———————

He woke to a ringing phone and an empty bed. Stumbling around looking for his iPhone, he realized it was the land line, and it took him a minute to get his bearings. He finally managed a fuzzy, "Hullo."

"Will, it's Merilee. Are you okay?"

"Yes, of course, why?"

"I couldn't reach your cell phone." As she spoke, he made his way to the closet to look through his clothes, and found it in a pocket, dead.

"I just found it. Long day. I forgot to charge it. Sorry. What's up?"

"Have you seen a newspaper today?"

"No. Just woke up." He looked around for any sign of Charlotte and walked downstairs. No signs of life. The newspaper was still folded up and on the hall table. He found a note in the kitchen.

Andy and I went to church. Needed it. Xoxo

"Things are heating up with the media," Merilee said.

Will opened the newspaper but didn't see any front-page headline. "Where are you getting this?"

"John Price has been fielding calls from reporters and couldn't reach you, so turned to me. We maybe should have had him in the command meeting yesterday, so he had some background."

"You're right. We should have had Public Relations with us." Will had thought they had some time to get ahead of this before needing to make a statement to the press. "What do we know about the media coverage exactly?" He took the paper with him and returned to the bedroom to retrieve his phone, plugging it into the charging station in the bedroom.

"Not too much. Names of companies affected have not been released. But one mid-level manager at Enger Pharmaceuticals confirmed the company was operating on crisis procedures."

Will found the reference on the inside of the paper, noting almost word for word what Merilee had just told him. "I'll call John and take it from here." He saw his phone start to come to life at the charging station. Time to move. "Listen, Merilee, I think I'll be staying at the office for a few nights. Could you make sure housekeeping puts some fresh towels and bedding in my suite? The couch will do if I can have a shower there."

He called John but had to leave him a voice mail. "Hang tight. I'll brief you, and we'll develop a statement in an hour. Heading to the office." He took a five-minute shower, dressed, and put some clothes in a carry-all. He guessed the next seventy-two hours would be crucial and wanted to be on top of it.

He plugged his phone into the car charger after noting several calls from the CEO of the Global Healthcare Association, the conference organizer, and one from Clark.

He called Clark back from the car. He held his breath

through the update, not sure what he wanted to hear. With Clark's words, 'No change, no ability to communicate. Heavily sedated and on a ventilator,' he exhaled slowly before he spoke. "What does that mean for his wife? She's gonna want to be with him. What will they tell her?"

"Clearly, she should visit him. As upsetting as it may be for her to see him in this condition . . ."

"Because?" Will needed to be sure.

"He won't respond to her presence. It's tough for families."

Will considered how hard that might be for her, and then thought about Danny, who was around the same age as his daughter, Tish. *Will Andrea have him visit?* He considered what he would do in this situation. Would he want Tish to visit him and risk her being traumatized or forced to put aside any fear she had to sit by his bedside? His eyes clouded over at the scenario. *Clearly, Tish should visit him. Is that selfish? Is Chet selfish or selfless? What do I really know about Chet's character now?*

He went to a Starbucks drive-through to get coffee and a couple of sandwiches to tide him over and was on the speakerphone in his office with John shortly after. He was scrolling through news websites and listening to John catalog the various inquiries he had received. John never used a sentence when he could use a paragraph. Will cut in.

"Were the inquiries about the hack overall or about how BioteKem, specifically, is handling the threat of business interruption?"

"Definitely the hack overall. The better reporters had researched past attacks and saw your name as a recent speaker addressing cybersecurity in biotech, so it didn't take them long to make a connection. They're looking for a local angle. There's been an uptick in threats in healthcare, the industry is starting to get stressed, and they want a quote or story idea about what happens next."

"Nothing about Chet yet?"

"No."

"Okay, then, I think we want to give them a narrative of responsibility taken. Something like this: 'BioteKem, a leader in global heath and innovator . . . yada yada yada . . . is taking this cyberattack extremely seriously and already working upstream with its partners internationally to protect from any business interruption due to undue stress. The company will be cooperating with the health-care authorities to assess risks to our clients and the patients. Protecting their well-being is our highest goal.'"

"I'd rather not be interviewed on this." Will was adept at press contact but couldn't see an upside to being associated with the hack. "But play that how you need to. Let's try to protect Chet's privacy until the last moment. It's really not a story that should lead the news. It's totally unrelated to the hack story and not ours to share." *I need to call Andrea.*

"Got it."

"Thanks, John. I'm sorry I didn't think to include you yesterday in the battle planning. Should have . . . totally blew it. But I need you on this now, one hundred percent, okay?" Will knew how important an apology was. Showing humility was a leadership trait he was not afraid to use. He needed to own his mistake.

He called Andrea, and during the conversation, he pictured her disheveled appearance in the ER, wearing her dress shoes and nightgown under her trench coat. The nightmare wasn't over for her or for him. He shuddered. Her voice had been so low, he could hardly hear her.

"Yes, I saw him, but I don't think he saw me. I'm so scared, Will. What if—"

"He's in an excellent hospital. They'll take good care of him." He was trying to find a way to comfort her that didn't sound false. *How did they know what would happen?* "How's Danny?"

"I didn't take him with me. Not sure how he'll handle seeing him like this."

"I understand. I'm so sorry this is happening. I'm here if you need me."

Will tried to soothe her but couldn't quite thwart the worry about what Chet would say if given the chance. "Charlotte sends her love."

His office intercom lit up for the security line from the lobby. He picked up. The team was not coming in today, Sunday, but working from home on their assignments.

"Dr. Franklin, there's somebody here to see you?"

"Who is it?"

"Bella Davis. Do you want me to let her up?"

Will's palms began to sweat, and he could feel his heartbeat in his ears. *What is she doing here?*

CHAPTER 6

"Yes, let her up." He thought back to the icy stare she had given him Friday night, after his curt cancellation of their date. Not sure of her mood now, he considered having the guard turn her away, but if that went awry . . .

The entire floor was empty. He left his office to meet her in the foyer by the elevator bank. He didn't want her in his personal space. He was leery, but not sure why. He didn't have control of this relationship. And yet, despite himself, he felt an urge he couldn't deny.

The elevator doors opened. She stepped out. Dressed in a sheepskin coat over leggings and high leather boots, she presented more like a model hung over after a weekend of partying than the persona of a research scientist. But that's what the initial attraction had been for him. With her morning-after hair haphazardly clipped back, she hurriedly took off thick glasses and put them in her pocket. She looked him straight in the eye.

"I figured you might be here on a Sunday trying to sort things out, and I didn't want things to be weird between us."

Her voice was soft. Both of them shifted their weight, the sudden cancellation of what would have been a sexy night together an awkward memory between them.

"I've been walking around this block for an hour trying to get up my nerve to come in."

"I'm sorry about Friday night. I didn't know . . ." Will stopped. *How can I apologize to my fling about my wife showing up unexpectedly?*

"She's lovely . . . and I understand." She turned her head aside with a slight smile. "What a mess we're in, huh?"

Will's body stiffened. He wasn't sure what she meant. Was she referring to their relationship, the state of the world with cyberattacks now so common, or something else? He let the silence work.

Bella filled it, eventually, pulling at an earring. "Have you been in touch with the Enger Pharmaceuticals folks yet about the attack?"

His shoulders relaxed, and he finally smiled. "No, not directly. I'm going to call the CEO this afternoon. Had to get our own scanning started first. You?"

"No, but it sounds like the conference organizers are trying to canvass the participants about how widespread the damage is."

Her eyes searched his face.

What is she hunting for? He moved to neutral territory, hoping she would follow. "They must be looking to add value to their role."

"Ahh . . . maybe." She finally cast her eyes down, the staring contest over.

"Do they have a list of companies already cleared from damage? Given the timing, I would think that to be a difficult process—to get any validation at this point."

"Yes," she answered quietly.

He was about to ask her more, when she said, "Will, I slept with the Italian venture capitalist."

Will studied her face for a clue. *What did she expect his response to be?* "Ohhhh . . . kay."

She continued quickly. "Friday night, after you saw me in the bar, I . . . well, I needed some companionship."

Is that a tremor in her voice? Does she expect jealous outrage from me now? His confusion toward her was compounded by the guilt he felt for having in some way put her in this situation. Had he been with her, she wouldn't have slept with the Italian. If not for Charlotte . . . For the first time it occurred to him she may have misinterpreted his attentions beyond the mere dalliance. Had he given her clues this wasn't just a fling?

He knew little of her personal life. Both of their hookups had been brief and passionate, not conversation driven. He wondered if she had anyone in her life who truly cared for her.

"Bella, I'm so sorry. Sorry for all of it. Are you okay?"

The false note of her laugh couldn't hide the tearful eyes. "Hey, I'm sure I'll be fine. It's my own doing. I'm a big girl and can take care of myself." She pulled herself up tall. "Thanks for letting me come up, I wasn't sure you would, this being your personal space." She hugged herself. He saw a less confident version of Bella lift her eyebrows and then look away, as if acknowledging she was just a plaything and had been temporary at best. "I just didn't want to message you about this. Felt wrong."

Their eyes met, empathy and sympathy a common understanding.

"Good luck getting your company through any hiccups from the hack." Will said.

"Thank you." She pushed the elevator button several times and didn't look back. "Goodbye, Will."

He stood at the elevator doors and stared at the numbers lighting up until she was in the lobby. What a cad he was. He recalled the wounded look in Bella's eyes on Friday night. Seeing him with his wife must have driven home her own status with him or made her so jealous that she wanted to take revenge on him by sleeping with someone. Either way, she was gone now, but the whiff of danger at this close call gave him a slight buzz, and she stayed in his head.

He tried to work it off until evening. He got a call back from Sybil Moran, the CEO of the Global Healthcare Association, and requested they set up a link back to him on their findings of the cyberattack reach as they tallied it.

"Happy to do it." Sybil then steered the conversation closer to BioteKem. "I heard about Chet. Such upsetting news. I didn't even see him on Friday. Did you?"

Not even Merilee knew about his meeting with Chet on Friday. His eyes involuntarily moved to his locked desk drawer where he had stowed Chet's laptop and phone. He still hadn't had a chance to peruse anything on the devices that could explain Chet's threats. *Should I deny any meeting with Chet on Friday? Does it matter?* He decided on a half-answer. "Ahh, Chet and his wife were at the dinner Friday night but not close by. I assume you know that he's in the hospital?"

"Yes, we heard from the hotel that he went by ambulance from there early Saturday morning."

"Yes, he did." Will said crisply.

"Are you in contact with Mrs. Sutherland then?"

"Yes."

"Please send my best wishes for a speedy recovery, will you?"

"Of course."

His detour worked, but his paranoia got the best of him. He got up from his desk and realized how tense he was. His muscles ached. He gazed around the room and noticed a custodian had left a cart of fresh towels and bedding outside his office. He walked into the break room to grab a water and headed back to his office to open the locked drawer.

But first he called Charlotte. She answered immediately.

"Hi love, I've been waiting for your call. I'm so sorry about the cyberattack. Terrible for everyone. What does it mean for BioteKem?"

Her warm voice pulled him into a calm space, despite the task ahead. "It's been another busy day. Nice to hear your voice. How's Andy?"

"He's good. We're both missing you on a Sunday, though. When will you be home? Did you get anything to eat?"

"About that. I'm not coming home. It's constant incoming here, I'm afraid. And I need focused time to look over Chet's communications." *And I need to be alone for that task.*

"Oh, Will. Can't you set up here? We could give you total privacy."

"Stop, please. I'm going to need to be here to get BioteKem through this and staying here will just be better for all of us. It won't be for too long." His heart tightened at the thought of being away from her this way but was afraid she would intuit something watching him with Chet's devices. "If we lose data even for one clinical trial, it could be catastrophic, you know that. Don't fight me on this. I need you to understand and be in my corner. Just like always."

"I don't like it, Will." She sighed. "But okay."

Team Franklin was back on. She questioned him about clothes he needed and anything else from home that she should get delivered to the office.

"I called Andrea this afternoon. She seems shattered. Sounds like Chet is not doing very well, and it's heartbreaking for her to see him this way. I can't imagine it."

"It is unimaginable."

He ended the phone call and thought about the last words Chet had spoken to him, still echoing in his head . . . words he still couldn't comprehend.

CHAPTER 7

C omputer sleuthing wasn't Will's strong suit. He navigated
business reports easily but didn't have time for much else
and barely handled more than email. If he had needed to
find something, he would have had Merilee get someone
to do it. They had IT geniuses in house and contracts with
cybersecurity firms if they couldn't do something themselves.
He was so far away from any of that, it was laughable. To
think he could find anything in Chet's computer or phone
that would incriminate him or set his mind free was difficult
to grasp.

Yet Andrea had entrusted him with the devices, thinking
they were precious to the health of BioteKem, like passing on
the baton of power. It revealed how little Andrea understood
about the company or how limited Chet's involvement with
it had become. He wondered what Chet shared with Andrea,
who was twenty-five years his junior. Many might consider
her a trophy wife, chosen by the older male to signify his
virility. They would be wrong. It was truly a love match and
seemed to be a very strong marriage.

And now, Andrea was watching her husband fight for
his life. As sobering as it was, he needed to shake it off

and get back to the immediate tasks in front of him. Had Chet really threatened his job? Now just three days since that weird meeting, Will wasn't sure it was a viable threat. Perhaps Chet was already feeling the effects of the oncoming stroke, which had clouded his judgment. He should be spending his time supporting Andrea or digging deeper into his own company's risk assessment with the current cyberattack at hand.

But Andrea had handed him the devices. He felt honor bound to look. She anticipated there would be important communications to be dealt with regarding BioteKem and that Will was the best person to take care of business. He doubted he would find any time-sensitive messages needing to be addressed ASAP. He was exhausted and hadn't eaten all day.

He glanced over at the Starbucks sandwiches he had picked up that morning and the housekeeping cart piled with bedding for the couch. To keep faith with Andrea, he decided he would scroll through email from Friday until today for any urgent messages. To put his own mind to rest, he would check Chet's calendar for any emergency board meeting that had been scheduled for the next week. "Divide up the tasks and prioritize," words he had lived by his entire working life.

He opened both devices and realized the phone had powered off. He found the power cord from the case and plugged it in. Fortunately, the computer guy had powered the computer up and left the password for him. He got in easily. He assumed email was synchronized between the two, so he went to computer email first. He scrolled through the most recent, not that many since Friday, and no name jumped out at him. He'd look more carefully after he checked Chet's calendar. BioteKem's spring board meeting was scheduled for mid-April, which was entered into Chet's calendar. He paid particular attention to the last weeks of March.

A couple of things stood out. Chet was taking a spring vacation in two weeks, around Danny's school break. The only other reference to board activity appeared, as per usual: an executive committee meeting of the board, scheduled for one week before the April meeting. If Chet was scheduling an emergency board meeting, there was no evidence of it on his calendar.

Will laughed out loud, a near-hysteria laugh that surprised him. He let his body fold back into itself, pushed his chair back, and put his head between his knees. He took shallow breaths until his body calmed enough to go deeper. The wave of relief opened his psyche to the state of his body—starving.

He stood up and shook himself all over. With new equilibrium, he washed up and ate his sandwiches at the small conference table in his office. He turned on the TV to hear any late news. The cyberattack was gaining traction across all cable and network sources but nothing he didn't already know. He turned it to late night comedy in an attempt to unwind.

The security guard had made last rounds at 11:00 p.m., and the lighting in the hallway was turned down automatically. He started to grow sleepy while putting his bed together. He put the fresh towels in his private bath and hung up the clothes from his bag in his closet. With the office coming back to life tomorrow, he would use the company gym early in the morning to get ready for the next lap of the marathon. He had known once the production line in Italy was threatened that this was not a sprint. All systems would need attention to determine how far the tentacles of the cyberattack had reached.

But for now, he had some hope he wouldn't be going down a rabbit hole to discover what Chet had meant on Friday night. He was just getting comfortable on his couch when he had a moment of clarity.

Merilee! Chet wouldn't know the first thing about setting up an emergency board meeting. He would have asked her to set up any such meeting. And, she hadn't said anything about it.

For one irresponsible moment, he considered popping out of his nest to text Merilee. But instead, he got up and wrote a note to himself with top-of-mind tasks to do right away tomorrow. Sleep hygiene is what they called this, he remembered from his early years of trying to get the most efficiency into his day as possible.

"Don't clutter your mind at night with reminders for tomorrow. Write them down and sleep soundly."

He scribbled the three words that were on his mind, in no order of priority:

Merilee, Bella, Chet.

CHAPTER 8

The next forty-eight hours were a blur as Will tried to run a global operation with no clear road map to determine vulnerabilities to their data and secure their supply chain linkages. In addition, growing panic among tech and pharma led to shifting allegiances among known business competitors and stockholders concerned about their investments. Mixed messages from government and cybersecurity experts made everything more confusing.

He was constantly on conference calls with other companies to cooperate on inventory issues and with the government to request or respond to emergency use items needed across the United States.

It was endless and thankless, and Will loved it. Not the hack itself but the ultimate necessity for problem-solving that mattered. This wasn't about making money for the company. It was about working through the biggest cyber-attack his world had ever witnessed and being in a position of power to help.

In his time at BioteKem, Will had deliberately worked to build a dream team of the best and most capable people to lock his rise to the CEO suite. They were as resilient as any executives anywhere. But lack of transparency across biotech and pharma during this crisis was beginning to frustrate all of them. They needed a break—something to keep them going.

In the midst of a near-collective meltdown, Larry Weisman, general counsel, made an appearance. He rapped lightly on the glass of the conference room wall and gestured for Will to join him. Will saw everyone stare at the big man in the hallway. At 6'4" tall and nearing sixty, he still had the bearing and muscle of his college football days. He was an elusive figure to the team. He was not a presence on a routine basis, but they associated him with deal-making at the highest levels. He had been in the biotech game so long it was rumored he knew where all of the skeletons were buried and was not afraid to leverage this knowledge for BioteKem's benefit.

As Larry waited outside the room, formidable in his impeccable corporate attorney suit punctuated by a semi-mullet of graying hair a tad beyond his collar, Will made a gut decision to have him join the group to share what he had come to tell Will.

Nothing like a moment of reckoning to forge a forever bond for this team, whatever the news may be.

He beckoned Larry in. "I think this team deserves to know, when I know, what you found out." Will gave Larry a nod and he took the stage.

"Hello everyone." Larry's voice boomed as he remained standing and returned the knowing nod back to Will. "While you all have been working hard to keep things operational and limiting any damage due to this cybersecurity breach, Mr. Franklin has had me working back channels to get to the crux of the threat."

Larry paused to heighten the drama, then went on. "Just five minutes ago, I confirmed that Enger Pharmaceuticals has indeed received a ransom demand from parties yet unknown for $15 million."

A master at both timing and reading the room, Larry halted to allow for the gasps and other audible responses to die down.

Will prompted him to share the next bit. "And Enger Pharmaceuticals's response?"

Larry chuckled lightly. "Oh, they'll be paying up. The hackers have them in a vice—the longer this goes, the greater the chance the collateral damage to the industry will be more than Enger Pharmaceuticals can risk. I'm unsure of the timing just yet."

During the shared exhale that followed, Will stood. "Everyone, how about a break? When we reconvene, we can switch gears a bit. And remember, any ransom news is confidential at this point. Thanks, Larry."

The room was abuzz with adrenaline and caffeine. Will shook Larry's hand, and they walked out of the room together.

Larry's first words to his boss were, "Well that was fun."

Will made daily contact with Andrea to check on Chet who was hanging on but not showing any improvement.

"I get all choked up seeing him hooked to machines and needles. People tell me it's good for patients to hear your voice, but I don't know, it doesn't feel like he registers anything." Andrea sobbed softly.

Will hung up and immediately called Charlotte, who said, "Oh no. This is too much for her. Should I offer to take Danny?"

"If you could arrange to get some meals to her and maybe what she needs from the store? That may be the immediate action to take. Call her?"

"Yes, of course. I know she doesn't have family close by, but what about Chet's daughter? Do you think Andrea let her know about her dad?"

"Not sure. Tread lightly there, I know the daughter and Chet were not close. Not sure how Andrea relates to her, if at all."

"Wow, this sudden illness doesn't give a damn about family dynamics, does it?"

Her rhetorical understatement ended the call but not Will's worries.

Finally, he bowed to temptation and queried Merilee. "I'm trying to sort out if Chet left any loose ends that I should tie up. Did he call on you to do anything for him the week before he was hospitalized?"

"No, I haven't talked to Chet in several weeks. I didn't have anything active going on his behalf. Let me just look a little closer here." He imagined her scrolling through several accounts.

"Thanks. Let me know if you find anything."

———◈———

He didn't hear from Bella. But there was a bubble of tension lodged in his mind that caused his head to throb every time he replayed her visit to his office. He wished he could go back and erase everything to do with her.

He thought back to the January event when they met. A scientific meeting in Philadelphia had featured new therapeutic trials. Bella had been a keynote speaker the first morning. Will didn't know that or her at the time. He didn't arrive until late afternoon, just in time for happy hour. One of the meeting organizers, a researcher from Penn, had invited him.

"Good chance to take a look at the new talent, and I'd love to catch up with you," Rich Connet had pitched to him. He had early history with Rich, who had stayed on the academic track. Every once in a while, Will liked to take a peek at that world to see what he was missing.

He was to meet Rich in the conference venue lobby before they went to dinner.

The bar was off the lobby, and the social hour had been going for at least forty-five minutes. Will knew scientific types were known to be reserved, but when free booze flowed and stimulating new ideas were in the air, they could let loose. Will had been casually watching a circle of men orbit around a very attractive woman whose husky voice, when she spoke, seemed to stop any other conversation.

He wasn't close enough to hear what she was saying but it didn't sound like she was telling funny stories, more like talking science in a sexy way. These men were transfixed and leaning in to hear every word. He studied her. Under thirty, he guessed. Straight dark hair that she wore behind her ears, thick glasses balanced atop her head or twiddled in her hand on occasion. Brilliant green eyes and bright red lips. Nondescript clothing, a rather tall black outline. The only feminine feature was her silver earrings, catching the candlelight when she moved, and dangling to her collar.

"Hey Will!" Rich came down the steps from the mezzanine level of the hotel and enthusiastically met his friend. Rich followed Will's gaze to the group at the bar.

"I see you are becoming bewitched by our Ms. Davis, as well." Rich laughed. "Quite the talent. She mesmerized the crowd this morning at her talk about her new start-up. People are excited about it, actually."

"Really? What's the story?"

"Seems a rare talent. Stanford grad. Reminds me of you, a bit."

"How so?"

"Young, bright scientist with an entrepreneurial spirit. Ready to go places. Sound familiar?"

"Hmm . . . sounds interesting. Introduce me tomorrow?"

"Sure thing."

———◈◈◈———

His reverie was interrupted when Gil Strom, Enger Pharmaceuticals's CEO, returned Will's call.

"Well, it's done." Gil's voice sounded hoarse. "But it's only the tip of the iceberg. The next cyberbully or rogue state is right around the corner, waiting to extort all of us."

"Sorry this happened to you, Gil. The transaction is complete, then?" Will knew this was not the time to press his case on how different solutions were necessary. The man was the latest victim to grasp the only solution available— pay up or possibly go belly up. At least they would never publicly release the amount—that information was on an embargo status carefully orchestrated with the FBI.

"Afraid so, yes. But we are still waiting for some indication that our systems are fully operational, and we can retrieve our data."

With this confirmation, Will felt he could finally go home. He decided to surprise his family and quickly packed up his clothes.

"I'm home!" He gleefully shouted out a few minutes later when he stepped through the front door.

Silence.

Moments later, Andy rushed through from the kitchen, a milk mustache signaling the remnants of an after-school snack. He gave his dad a big welcome-home hug.

"You're home!"

"Where's your mom, big guy?" Will asked, as he peered over to the kitchen door, expecting to see Charlotte charge out to greet him.

"In the kitchen."

"Charlotte, I'm home." Will headed that way. He found

her with her head in the freezer and leaned into her to kiss her neck.

"Will, hi. You're home." She stayed on task with her groceries, dodging any contact. "Didn't expect you." Her voice was as chilly as the bag of peas in her hand.

"No, I decided to surprise you. Just caught a turning point in the attack recovery, and I took it as a sign that I could return home to a more normal existence. Missed you guys."

"Missed you, too, Dad. Come see what I built in my room while you were gone." Andy took him by the hand and led him to his room.

Will looked back at Charlotte, who didn't follow.

They had a quiet family dinner attuned to Andy's questions about why his dad was staying at the office.

"Did you sleep on the floor? Was it like a slumber party?"

Will was aware Charlotte's demeanor could be explained by a mother's impulse to allow Andy the spotlight—but that wasn't it.

After Will got Andy to bed, he found Charlotte curled up in a wing chair in the darkest corner of the great room, a cashmere throw over her shoulders, a glass of wine in her hand. He turned a lamp on and took a seat as close as possible, across from her.

"Charlotte, what's wrong?"

"I saw Andrea today." Her eyes met his quickly and locked.

Will's throat constricted. He fought through his paranoia to get out the most neutral words he could come up with. "How is she?" *Did Andrea tell Charlotte that Chet planned to fire me?*

"Not good." Charlotte's voice was unnaturally monotone. "We need to get somebody to chip ice in the Sutherlands' driveway. It's not safe. Not sure how much Andrea is tracking with day-to-day stuff. I brought food and told her I would tend to groceries for her for a while. She was grateful."

"We can do that."

"I had to pull my car up close to the back door in the icy driveway. Andrea was home alone. Danny was at school. She had been drinking and continued to do so while I was there. When I asked how she was, she said, 'I can't handle this. This is too much.'"

Charlotte's voice became almost robotic as she gazed beyond Will but continued to relay the conversation with Andrea.

"Assuming it was Chet's illness that was bothering her, I told her about his being in good hands, etc., but her eyes glossed over. She said she knew he was being taken care of, so I asked her if it was Danny. She had replied, 'Not really. Both Danny and I have noticed Chet's been off lately. Like, maybe hiding something. Not as close, not as loving, distant. Something big was on his mind.'

"I asked her if she tried talking to him about it, which she had, but he said she was imagining things. When I asked if she thought he was sick or he wasn't telling her something, she couldn't look at me directly. She kept sipping her drink, and then, as if she finally got her nerve up, blurted, 'I think he may have been having an affair.' She broke down in tears. I was dumbfounded and told her I always found the two of them to be made for each other, the epitome of the loving couple. I asked her why she thought Chet was having an affair.

"She laughed and then explained, 'The usual cliché. What everybody always says they should have picked up on after they find out their husband was wandering—no interest in sex with her, late meetings with colleagues that he didn't identify, a night or weekend away here and there over the past several months that were unexpected and never explained.

"She told me about one weekend that came up at the last minute and interfered with a ski getaway they were going to take as a family. He had to fly to Detroit on business. But when he got home and Danny asked about his trip, he had said Cleveland was good. There was also a trip to New York City for some hush-hush BioteKem deal that was scuttled at the last minute—Presidents' Day weekend. He was ticked off about it but wouldn't tell her why."

Charlotte sipped her wine and closed her eyes for a moment before she turned back to stare into his eyes.

Will's heart felt like it moved to his throat. His body closed down, as if glued to the chair. His mind was in turmoil. His worry that Andrea had told her Chet was about to fire him was so off base he was stunned. He commanded the gears in his brain to shift to this now more dangerous situation—the weekend in NYC. *Does Charlotte suspect I'm having an affair?*

Charlotte's voice was now a whisper. "Andrea said she was halfway wondering if she should ask the hospital staff if there'd been a woman trying to visit. Maybe then she'd know. I tried to comfort her as best I could, but she was very upset." Charlotte's voice quavered briefly.

Will got up to go to his wife, but she put her arm out to signify he should not approach her.

"Will, you were in New York City Presidents' Day weekend. If the whole deal got scuttled, why did you still go?"

Charlotte was now cool, calm, and direct, as she always was when determining their next move.

Will took a deep, ragged breath and closed his eyes. "The meeting was cancelled, but I went anyway." His voice was a rough whisper. "I met a woman and spent the weekend with her."

Charlotte sat like a stone, finally asking, "What woman?"

"Bella Davis, a biotech up and comer who has a new company. She asked me to mentor her—"

"Mentor her? Is that what you did? That weekend in New York City? Did you spend the weekend with this Bella Davis, mentoring her?"

Will said nothing. She repeated her question and demanded an answer, loudly. "Tell me Will, what happened between you and this woman that weekend?"

Finally, he shook his head. "No, I didn't mentor her. I slept with her. And I regret it more than I thought possible. It was a huge mistake. I'm so sorry."

Charlotte stood so quickly, she was unsteady on her feet, allowing him to try again to approach her. "Charlotte, it's over. Please forgive me."

But she pulled herself out of reach. "Stop. Don't touch me. I've heard enough. I'm going to bed. Alone."

She left him unmoored, without any solace. As he attempted to follow her, she commanded, "Either go back to the office or sleep on the couch, but stay away from me."

Her eyes were so cold, he pivoted to a dead stop. He felt like an actor in a play that she was directing, calling "cut" when he was prepared to play out the scene, leaving him without a script for the next act.

He was gutted. He paced the great room, berating himself for his foolishness in betraying the wife he cherished, the wife who had shared his life as a partner in every way for the best part of twenty years. *What have I done to her? To us?*

Finally, he began problem-solving. He knew only the truth would lead him back to his wife. *How did I get here?* His mind went back to the beginning. Back to the January meeting in Philadelphia.

Will had been intrigued watching Bella entertain a throng of admirers in the bar while waiting for Rich Connet, who had agreed to introduce him to her. But Bella beat him to it. When he picked up his name badge at registration the next morning, she had left a note to meet her at the coffee break and signed it, "Big fan of yours, Bella."

At first annoyed that she would make the assumption it was a priority for him to meet her, he had to admire her chutzpa. He was there to network with academia, and many people wanted to have time with the president of BioteKem. He had to admit she was the most attractive fan he was likely to meet there. It took him awhile to find the meeting room she had suggested, which was away from the crowd.

"Ms. Davis, I presume?" He stretched his hand out to her to shake.

During the first session of the morning, he had read the program description for yesterday and scanned her bio. PhD Stanford, Oxford scholar, specialty biochemistry, immunology. Start-up currently in product design.

"Dr. Franklin, it's such a pleasure to meet you. I was so excited when I saw your name on the list of attendees."

She took his hand and kept it. Dressed in black again, she wore a clingy scarf draped over her torso cinched at the waist with an alligator belt. Her hair was pulled into a low ponytail.

Somehow, the combination of flattery and clear sex appeal worked quickly on Will. He wanted to kiss the soft hollow of her neck, which peeked out between her scarf and the same dangly silver earrings from last night. He didn't take his hand away until she finally let it go.

"I understand you gave a good talk yesterday. Tell me about your science."

"Happy to do that, maybe when we have more time. In summary, I'm about to change the world with a new way to control diabetes."

"Oh." Will laughed. "I see you aim high. I'd love to hear more about it."

"I've got to warn you. I've got you on the top of my list of potential mentors. Your early academic work leading to the breakthrough for a new asthma treatment is textbook for the trajectory I want to take with my own career. Brilliant work."

Her charisma focused on him alone, and he liked it. "Well, that's nice of you to say. I do take an interest in molding young talent when I can." He blushed when his thoughts turned to how he would mold Bella Davis, in a physical sense.

She leaned in a little. "I'll take that as a possible yes! I'm thrilled that you would consider taking me on."

Two hotel staff wheeled in a service cart, interrupting what was fast becoming a steamy situation, effectively stopping whatever was about to happen. With the door open, they heard the speaker announce the start of the next session.

"Listen, I have to leave the meeting now, but I'm going to be in Boston in a couple of weeks to meet a potential investor. We're in the final stage of our first equity call. Dr. Franklin, is it possible we could meet when I'm in your town?" She pulled out a card and leaned into him, her perfume filling his senses.

"Sure, let's make that happen." Will gave her his own card without the usual warning about how hard it was to get on his calendar. "And call me Will."

He admired the gentle swish of her slim hips and toss of her hair as he watched her walk away. She turned to give him a lover's smile before exiting the room.

That's how it happened.

CHAPTER 9

■■■■■■■■■■■■■■■■■■■

Will's body jerked as he woke up to a muffled grating noise. *Garage door?* He peeked at unfamiliar surroundings and tried to determine where he was. His head throbbed as he stood up in his boxers and T-shirt. *Ahh, the builder's nanny suite.* It had recently been done over in more neutral colors for its reincarnation as a guest suite, mostly for Oliver, Charlotte's widowed father. Ollie hadn't used it yet, but it was ready for him. Will made a mental note to consider the timing of garage use during his visits, then realized with a jolt he had work to do to make sure he was still living here by then.

Will had been so sound asleep, it took him a moment to remember the reason he had slept there. He ran out of the room to the front door and was ready to fling it open and stop his wife from driving away when the door opened, and Andy walked in.

"Morning Dad, I forgot my trombone for my lesson today." He picked it up from the floor by the entry. "Mom says you have to go back to the office for a few more nights. Good luck fighting off the bad guys. Love you. Bye."

Will caught the door before Andy slammed it and glimpsed Charlotte as she checked to make sure Andy buckled his seat belt. Her eyes lifted briefly to the door, but if she saw him, she didn't acknowledge him as she drove off.

He backed away from the door and almost tripped over his overnight bag, still full of dirty clothes from his days away. Fuzzy from little sleep, he couldn't face the day without coffee, and headed to the kitchen. He had to hunt around to make a fresh pot; he couldn't remember the last time he made his own. While he waited, he found the note Charlotte had left for him on the counter.

W—I need some time alone—go back to the office for a few more nights—C

His body trembled. *A few nights.* It had been nearly dawn when he'd moved on from beating himself up for getting involved with Bella and finally faced the truth—he would be lost without Charlotte, his north star from the beginning.

What a geek he was as a wunderkind in his PhD program. He had stuck to the books—truly driven to research for solutions to help people with rare diseases. His smarts and willingness to do whatever was necessary to support the work did not go unnoticed by ambitious professors who pulled him into their labs. His genius was his ability to find the missing piece of a puzzle and to articulate it to a curious audience. After postdoc work at several prestigious institutions, he led a team to discovery of a breakthrough drug cocktail for asthmatics. The hoopla of the discovery was a game-changer for him.

The senior academics gained acclaim and monetary reward. And Will got a promotion to full professor. It was Charlotte, a public relations associate for the university at the time, who saw his potential. After interviewing several team members and the ranked academics in the limelight, she doubled back to him.

He was flattered when she suggested they meet for a drink.

"So, your team gives you all the credit for the discovery, did you know that?" She told him he was the rare talent, and that the academic higher-ups were taking advantage of him. "Off the record, you should leave these guys to years of academic gridlock and move into the biotech industry. Monetize your talent. You just drove a team to discovery of a product that will make life easier for patients everywhere and make millions."

He hadn't ever thought about his talent as something to use differently. But it was her allure and confident use of the word "monetize" that caught his attention. And it was her pursuit of him as a suitor that turned his heart, then his head to a new path. At first, she led the way. But after his first taste of big money and the perks that went with it, which they both learned to enjoy, he saw how easy it was and how right she had been. He found his way. But it was Charlotte who set the direction.

Now, when he thought back to listening to her last night, he shuddered. When she finally asked him about that weekend, he was eager to tell her everything. She was his partner. His obsession to unburden himself was almost a physical craving, even as he knew he would hurt her terribly in doing so. *What a mess!*

In the bright light of a new day, he decided to chase that last image of Charlotte away and move forward. She asked for time—she didn't kick him out. Eking out hope, he decided he was a lucky man. The least he could do is give her what she said she needed. He would give her time, as much as he could manage. But not too much. He needed her. He would call her tonight.

The cyberattack was not over. He needed to keep his focus there.

After showering, he heard a text come in. He quickly checked, hoping it was Charlotte. But it was from Merilee.

FYI, I did get a text from Chet Friday morning asking me to call him Monday morning. Didn't say what about.

That message made it hard to focus only on the cyber-attack.

As Will drove to the office, he took a call from John Price. After the ransom request was announced, the media was abuzz with curiosity about any other players who were being hit up for cash or bitcoin. Fortunately, none of BioteKem's proprietary systems had been infected, but the far-flung software systems that linked many of the biotech suppliers to pharma were all offline until their firewalls were deemed sufficient to hold.

"They want a direct quote this time, Will. I have one ready if you approve it."

Will approved what John read to him with a slight change, but his main priority was to get back to Chet's devices to see what else he could be missing now that he knew Chet had asked Merilee to call him. The worst-case scenario was that Chet was going to ask her to schedule the emergency board meeting he had planned in order to fire Will, as she was the admin liaison to the board. However, Chet now had more activity with BioteKem's Foundation on a routine basis. Perhaps he wanted Merilee to do something related to that. *Who else knows about Chet's plan?*

At the office, he rejoined his team in the conference room, still set up as a command center, with each of them on their own computer but huddled together for quick communication. The lively banter in the room lightened his mood.

"Wow," he remarked. "What a difference a day made for this group."

"I think it was more likely the $15 million that Enger Pharmaceuticals paid that did it!" Joy Meadows from IT said, and everyone laughed. Joy added, "We're still not sure all of the data can be restored, but that process has begun. Will, what's your thinking now about all the work you started to get biotech to wake up to the threat of cyberattacks getting bigger and more frequent? Is it going to finally have its moment?"

Will smiled for the first time in days. "Yeah, actually. You may be right. The unpopular position I took may get some traction now. Fifteen million is an amount that does get attention, doesn't it?" His warning had resulted in immediate pushback from his colleagues across the industry for describing the big bogeyman of cyberattacks as a threat that called for a collective response. "Do we want to get picked off one-by-one or come up with a defense that will work for all of us?" But as it required cooperation among competitors and big bucks, it was not an easy sell.

A few hours later, he finally took out Chet's phone.

He chided himself for not checking text history earlier; he would have seen the text to Merilee. Chet hadn't texted her other than that one time, within a three-week period. Now he looked more carefully. His history had a few chains, but nothing of note, mostly just to confirm meetings or locations and a few reminders.

Chet's email was filled with industry news; he was on numerous Listservs. Emails included vacation planning with his travel agent, and Will made a mental note to talk to Andrea about cancelling the trip; and some routine business with his broker—looked like they were doing some planning for his impending retirement. Will reviewed a few of the messages to see if he could determine an exact date but found nothing other than "as per our plan." Also, messages from his attorney, regarding the discussed revision of his estate plan, but no detail.

Will was beginning to feel like a voyeur, and even though Andrea had handed him the computer and the task, he didn't want to overstep. He checked his approach. *Is this what a friend does for a friend when asked by his wife? How about when the friend was his boss? How about when the friend was a boss who had threatened his job?* He framed it that way and puzzled through his thinking.

It seemed reasonable to prioritize any communication for pending company business, then to peruse time-sensitive personal communication, for instance, the vacation and any current financial or legal items that needed to be addressed.

It was a reasonable approach, which also allowed him to address his worry about any special board meeting in the works. He found no evidence of a board meeting or that anyone knew it was Chet's plan to call such a meeting to fire him. The longer it went, the more ridiculous it seemed. Chet was not himself that Friday.

Andrea returned yesterday's call. "Sorry Will, I meant to call you earlier, but time got away from me."

"How are you?"

"Exhausted. And not as hopeful. The doctors are considering brain surgery to relieve the swelling in his brain." Her voice was weak.

Will tried to comfort her, "I'm so sorry you are going through this. I'm trying to figure out what more I can do to help."

"You've been great. And please thank Charlotte for the visit and grocery delivery. That'll keep us for a bit."

"I hate to keep you on the phone, but I have a couple of things I need to ask you about. I've had a chance to go through Chet's phone and computer to check for any urgent pending company biz, and we're okay on that front. All is taken care of."

"Oh, good. Thanks."

"But the spring vacation to St. Bart's that you all had planned. I'm thinking I should call the travel agent and cancel. Is that okay with you?"

She moaned, then a muffled sob. "Yes, please. I can't really believe any of this is happening." She paused. "You didn't see anything that would be upsetting to the company on his computer, then?"

"No, should I have?"

"I don't know. He was upset about something that Friday but wouldn't tell me about what. Said it would work its way out. Thought you may find something that would explain it." Another moment of silence on the line, then a rush of words. "I gotta go. I'm texting you Danny's cell phone number in case you need to reach us. I did let certain friends know what was going on with Chet, but if you get any calls or messages to his phone or computer, feel free to let them know what's going on."

Upset about something that Friday. Her words echoed in his head. *Yes, he was upset that he had decided to fire me! But did he tell anyone else?* Another wave of nausea grabbed him just as he thought he could start to relax.

He circled the executive floor of offices, popped into a few for one-to-one problem-solving, and stopped to get a soft drink and snack in the break room before pulling Chet's phone and computer out again.

He had checked text and email, but now focused on phone calls.

He jotted down three names on a piece of paper to study: Hayes Miller, Robert Gornick, and Robin Warren. It was slow and tedious work to check these names against those copied on group emails from the Listservs or the personal ones. But any of the names could be explained as a golfing buddy, or industry associate, or even the assistant or associate of the attorney or broker he was working with. He couldn't imagine this was how the forensic cyber investigators did it, but it was what he thought to do.

Noting Chet's son was a frequent caller, he decided to check on Danny, who answered on the first ring. Chet was close to his son, and Will knew this must be a tough time for him.

"Hey, Dan. It's Will Franklin calling. How are you doing?" It seemed so lame to ask this question. He was startled by the voice of a young man on the line. He had only met Danny once, when he was a couple years younger.

"Okay, I guess. It's a strange time."

They chatted for a bit about Chet, and Danny relayed how hard it was to see him on a vent, when he finally visited.

"Do you have what you need there at the house?" Will imagined a home in disarray, an adolescent growing up fast. He couldn't imagine his daughter, Tish, also age fifteen, in this position.

"Yeah, I do. Mom wants me to keep going to school. Do you think I should?"

"Well, I think that depends on how you feel about going." He realized Danny wasn't sure how to act in such a limbo state. "Only you can decide."

"That's kinda what I was thinking." Danny's stronger voice seemed to respond to the validation by an adult.

"Anything else on your mind?"

After a slight hesitation, Danny finally spoke. "Ahh, Dad's daughter, Amy, called. I don't know her well, and I don't want to upset Mom about it, I was wondering if . . ."

"You want me to call her?"

The sigh was audible. "That would be great. I'll text you her number. Thanks."

Will guessed he had just rescued Danny from a more complicated interaction than he might be up for. He was happy to do it, but wondered what type of family dynamic he was walking into.

CHAPTER 10

The first night without the security of Charlotte's unwavering love and support, Will's mind kept flitting to other sleepless nights due to fussy newborns, jet lag due to relocations to other time zones, and nights in the ICU waiting room while Charlotte's mom was in her final hours. All shared with Charlotte. Now he had put the future with her at risk. He physically yearned for her body next to him, her limbs entwined with his.

He tried calling her several times, but she didn't pick up. Each time he left a voice mail apologizing and declaring his love. He considered calling Tish at boarding school just to chat but didn't think he could handle his emotions. He couldn't take a chance on what Charlotte might have told her. She had asked for time, and he would honor that. However, he wasn't sure for how long he could hold out.

The following morning, he went for a run along the Charles River to get a change of scenery and clear his mind. Away from his workspace, he freed his mind to wander a bit, to tick through whatever came forward, forcing himself to block the obvious personal peril he was in with his wife.

Updates on Chet weren't good. The hemorrhagic stroke had resulted in a burst artery, and they were waiting for him to stabilize enough to perform surgery to deal with it. He wanted Chet to recover for many reasons. He liked the man and wanted him around. Even though Will was ready to run the company on his own, he liked knowing Chet would still be in his universe as a respected mentor and friend. But more than that, Will needed Chet to get out of this alive so he could sort things out with him, let that whole crazy conversation go, and chalk it up to some sort of prestroke delusion. Instead, it lingered in his mind, along with his confusion over Bella.

Finished with his run and still restless, he considered driving out to his house. Would the romantic gesture be the right thing, or would Charlotte feel disrespected? He decided to text Merilee to send her flowers, the pink roses that she loved.

Back at the office, he showered and pulled out the phone number for Chet's daughter, Amy. He tried to recall what he knew about her. Not much. Chet never talked about his first marriage or the death of his wife, which Chet had described as unexpected. In hindsight, Will wondered if that was code for suicide. He knew it was not a happy marriage, and Chet did not have a close relationship with his daughter. The daughter had called Andrea, which meant something he couldn't possibly know.

"Good morning. This is Will Franklin, calling for Amy Sutherland."

"Well, there's nobody here by that name, but you are speaking to Amy Washburn. Sutherland was my maiden name. How may I help you?"

Formal yet not unwelcoming, she got her message across.

"I'm calling on behalf of Andrea and Dan Sutherland. You called their house sometime yesterday, I believe."

"Yes, to inquire about my father." She paused. "And who are you again?"

"Will Franklin. I work with Chet at BioteKem and have tried to offer Andrea support this past week."

"What type of support is it that Andrea needs exactly?"

"I helped her get Chet to the right hospital and have stayed close at her request."

Will tried to decipher whether she was being snarky or just curious and remained guarded.

"Okay, okay, I get it. You're trying to protect Andrea from me. I mean no harm. I'm just trying to find out what's going on with Dad!" Amy let off some reserved steam finally at the circumstance she found herself in. "How is he?"

Boundaries understood, Will warmed up considerably. "I understand totally. Let me give you the rundown."

"Yes, please. I haven't spoken to Andrea for years, or Danny for that matter, so me calling out of the blue may have been startling, but this is my dad we're talking about."

"Your dad fell in the bathroom the night we were all staying at the Intercontinental Boston Hotel a week ago Friday. It was the gala night of the Annual Global Health-care Summit, and BioteKem is a sponsor. He was taken by ambulance to Mass General Hospital and admitted for a possible concussion or head injury."

"Was he diagnosed with a traumatic brain injury then?"

"Not immediately. They did some scans, and it seems more like a hemorrhagic stroke. His breathing was impaired enough to require ventilator management. But he's in a good hospital. They are doing everything they know to do to treat him."

"Oh my God. How's Andrea doing with all of this? And Danny?"

"It's very hard for them both. How did you find out about your dad? Did Andrea let you know?"

"No, one of my dad's friends on your board called to let me know he was in the hospital. I guess there was an internal communication sent Monday?"

Will took a risk. "Do you mind telling me whether you were in contact with your dad at all?"

"I don't mind, as you sound like someone he trusts. And evidently Andrea and Danny do as well." She forged ahead. "I'm not sure he told them, but my dad and I were in contact of late. He wanted to breach the divide between us, so to speak. After all of these years, I was open to it."

"Hmmm. Did Andrea know?"

"I don't know. There was no reason to keep it a secret, but I imagine Dad wanted to get it a bit further on before he made any announcements."

"Announcements?"

"Oh, just a figure of speech. I know he was getting ready to retire and put his affairs in order, so I assume he wanted to get his family sorted as well. I give him tons of credit for reaching out. There was a lot of misunderstanding between us around my mother's illness and suicide that had to be sorted. But he hung in there for many tough conversations."

"I see. Your dad did like to pull people together when he could."

"Yes, and I resisted it for years." Her voice dropped. "I love him."

"I'm sorry about what's happened, Amy."

She started to rush her words. "I have to see him. I'll make my own plan to visit when neither she nor Danny are at the hospital. Regardless of whether Andrea knew that we were in contact and rebuilding our relationship, it's too much to push myself in right now."

He heard a long exhale before she asked him to stay in touch.

He agreed. Before signing off, Amy made a final plea.

"I'm a nurse. I'm not sure you knew that. I would be in a position to help interpret the potential complications if it came to that. My heart goes out to Danny. It's too much for a fifteen-year-old. I know. I have a fifteen-year-old myself."

"As do I."

Despite the life-and-death nature of their situation, they both laughed knowingly.

———————————⬦———————————

Will was caught up into the evening, with various players in a tense discussion regarding whether Enger Pharmaceuticals should have been advised not to pay the ransom. Some argued now that the entire industry was a top target of cybercriminals and the ransom amounts were growing exponentially, the question of paying the ransom should be considered and not inevitable.

"The only way biotech and pharma will be safer is to develop systems that are as impenetrable as we can make them. Yes, it is a very expensive pathway, but clearly less expensive collectively than wearing a big bullseye as fat cats willing to pay bigger and bigger ransom demands." Will doubled down on the position he publicly aired a year before this latest demand. Sybil's trade association was trying to keep the various parties talking about how to handle this delicate issue. The government wanted no company to pay . . . ever. However, corporations had immediate operational requirements, and while it was the right decision—not to give in to extortion, it was hard to do.

Larry Weisman was a proponent of a collective hard line by all in order to keep the industry together in defending its intellectual property from pirates. He'd taken a strong stance on that position within the biotech legal community. Both Larry and Will knew it would take more time to get the industry behind this position—and this time, Enger Pharmaceuticals had already bowed to the pressure. Unspoken but understood between them—BioteKem, if faced with that decision right now, would do the same thing.

Larry and Will huddled after the conference call ended, challenging one another on how to get their position moved forward.

"It's gonna take a humongous IT plan and the courage for a few big companies to declare—make a pact," Larry stated. "In some ways, this large demand to Enger Pharmaceuticals may help move the discussion forward for everybody."

"Agreed. Hard to expect Gil to take the bullet on his own." Will remembered the defeat in Gil's voice when he had talked to him just days before.

Larry rose from his chair in the conference room and stretched. "It's late. I'm heading out. You?"

"No, gotta do a bit more here." The urge to go home was strong, but instead he said, "See you tomorrow."

It was after 8:00 p.m. He decided to walk down a few blocks to a nearby pub to get a sandwich. As he walked, he considered how long before Charlotte would allow him to apologize in person and try to make things right. Now at almost forty-eight hours, he knew tomorrow would be his breaking point. He thought back to his conversation with Amy and how if things were normal with Charlotte, he would be discussing the situation with her. He missed the intimacy of problem-solving together, and all of the day-to-day interaction he took for granted. *I'm a fool.*

He took out his phone to catch up on the past five hours and sipped his beer.

His heart fluttered when he saw a VM from Charlotte. Her soft voice brought tears to his eyes. "I know you've left many messages, but I'm not quite ready to hear you out yet. I'm still trying to get my equilibrium after . . . well, you know. I just never expected it . . . never for us . . . I'll let you know."

He immediately called her back but no luck. His heart was beating so fast he took a series of shallow breaths to try to regulate his body. Time had run out. He needed to get to her now.

He searched his phone for any other messages from Charlotte. Nothing. There was an email from Merilee with the subject line that stopped his heart completely.

Family in Florida.

"FYI. Able to get Charlotte and the kids on a PM flight. They should arrive at her dad's sometime late tonight. I assumed you wanted me to deliver the flowers to her there, so have arranged for an AM delivery tomorrow. Sorry you are missing this spring getaway. Charlotte understands completely. She knows the cyberattack needs your full attention. I'll see you in the office tomorrow, Merilee."

"Can I get you anything else, sir?" the server repeated. Will looked down at his untouched sandwich and started to shake his head, then quickly responded, "Uh, could you wrap this to go?" and pulled out his credit card to settle up and get to Port St. Lucie ASAP. *Time's up.*

While the server packaged his sandwich, Will found a flight out at 7:00 a.m. the next morning and booked it. He went back to the office and spent a couple of hours getting some paperwork sorted and had a pile on Merilee's desk for her attention the next morning. Calendar management was easy as they were operating in crisis mode. All routine meetings were on hold until the cyberattack was under control. Fortunately, his team was now heading in a direction already set, and he could leave for a few days confident they would carry on without him.

By midnight he was home and packing, with a car and driver scheduled for a 5:00 a.m. pick up.

He caught a few hours of sleep, knowing he had to be sharp to face the most critical meeting of his life.

Two things slowed his departure the next morning. *Where in hell are my swimming trunks?* A photograph of his family on the beach near Ollie's house in Florida screamed out to him about what he was at risk of losing. He finally gave up the hunt, and as he walked through the kitchen on his way out, he saw a large manilla envelope on the table with a note from Charlotte attached.

Will, Andrea gave this to me, for you, the other day.
I forgot it was in my car.

He scooped up the envelope and his bag as the driver rang the bell for the second time, his Chet antenna now on high alert. He examined the contents and cover letter. It appeared to be a routine report on a company seeking research money from the foundation. As per protocol, the company's name was x'd out to provide for blind assessment, and the name of the person assigned to review the company was unknown to Will.

He breathed easier. This was Chet's wheelhouse, which he enjoyed. Funding new research companies was something he was happy to have the time to do now that he was freed from the everyday grind of running the company. He scribbled a note on the envelope asking Merilee to get this to Larry Weisman and asked the driver to drop the envelope off at BioteKem after he got Will to the airport. Any second thoughts about leaving Chet's devices unattended disappeared.

Instead, he turned his attention to Ollie.

Will had always enjoyed a good relationship with his father-in-law. Distant, but forged by a mutual respect of manly understanding of the role of a father and breadwinner. Will recalled Oliver testing him a bit to make sure his daughter would be well taken care of, in the traditional sense. Once Will started to make big money, he and Charlotte relocated Ollie and Charlotte's mom to a new house built for them in Port St. Lucie, within a retirement community with all of the amenities. It provided a getaway spot for the family to visit their only grandparents. Now that Ollie was widowed, it was a great supportive spot for Ollie on his own.

He was pretty sure Charlotte hadn't confided in anyone, including her father, about Will's betrayal. But Ollie was a smart old guy and had seen a lot of life in his day. Will's throat tightened at the idea Ollie might guess Will had been unfaithful to his beloved daughter.

He shook his fear off to focus on how to make things right. As he boarded the plane, his thoughts turned to Charlotte.

CHAPTER 11

The warm Florida air was a balm for Will's psyche when he walked through the revolving doors at the Palm Beach airport and stretched his legs while he waited for his Uber. He took off his sports jacket and pulled out his sunglasses. He hoped his weary body would accept a blast of adrenaline to help him through this all-important meeting with his wife. *Almost there.*

Fortunately, midday traffic was moving; his eyes scanned the oceanfront homes and extravagant boats meant to satisfy every whim in this playground. Same ocean, but different world from the work-a-day harbor view he was used to in Boston.

The Uber pulled up behind a florist's van just arriving at Ollie's house. Will quickly settled with the driver and jumped out to intercept the delivery. With pink roses in clammy hands and a bright but shaky smile, he rang the bell. He rang it two more times. He was about to head to the backyard when Charlotte, pony-tailed and barefoot, appeared at the door.

Will inhaled sharply as she took one step back. Her hand flew to her face before she whispered, "You came."

Will caught a clear beam of love fighting through a film of watery eyes, a curtain of unmistakable hurt. She took another step back.

"Of course, I came. I can't stay away. I love you." He handed her the flowers. "These are for you. May I come in?"

She opened the door wider, and he followed her into the house. Silence. "Where is everybody?"

Charlotte moved into the great room and put the bouquet on an end table before she faced him, arms crossed and positioned behind a chair. "The kids and Dad went down to the clubhouse for a golf lesson." Her eyes bored into him. "This is a good time for you to state your case. I'm listening."

The script Will had prepared in the plane failed him. All he had was his guilt and regret. He had no way to make it pretty.

"Charlotte, I'm so sorry I was unfaithful to you, to us, to our family, and what we've built together. I would give anything to undue that fling—which didn't mean anything to me. I love only you. I can't believe I've risked it so foolishly."

Charlotte didn't flinch as Will sobbed. All she said was, "Why did you cheat?"

"I'm ashamed, Charlotte. I fell for the seduction of flattery from a young woman with promise. It was stupid, dangerous, and totally reckless on my part. It was in my power from the beginning to steer her request for mentoring to the right path or dismiss it entirely. I was weak and allowed my shallow ego to take over—and hurt her in the process." Will paused for a breath.

Charlotte's spine stiffened as she pointed at herself. "And what about hurting me? Did you think about me at all? What am I to you?"

"Oh God, Charlotte." Will moved toward her. "You are everything to me and have been from the beginning."

He was closing the distance between them, but she backed away. "All I can do is apologize and ask for your forgiveness. I would be lost without you. She means nothing to me. It was just a fling. And it's totally over."

"How do I know that? How can I ever trust you again?" Charlotte's steely words drilled into his core.

Will was about to answer, "You have my word," when he realized that now meant nothing to his wife.

CHAPTER 12

The arrival of Ollie and the kids interrupted the standoff. "Daddy, we didn't think you'd be able to come!" Tish ran ahead to wrap her arms around him with Andy following closely behind. "I was worried I wouldn't get to see you during my school break!"

Will closed his eyes and breathed in the essence of his kids; he would never take it for granted again. "Hey, I'm here, I'm so happy to be here with all of you." A tear escaped as he scanned the room for his wife, who had disappeared.

"Great to have you here. Charlotte had us thinking that crazy hack attack would keep you away." Ollie picked up Will's bag and headed to the bedroom he and Charlotte used during their visits.

"We're home to get our swimming suits on. Grandpa said he'd take us down to the beach. Will you come?" Andy asked.

Will looked up at Ollie, who was sagging. "Will, if you're up for it, I'll stay here and take a little nap. I'm afraid keeping up with these two tired me out. And that vertigo medicine doesn't help."

"You have vertigo, Ollie?" Will inquired.

"Yeah. That's why I couldn't come up to Boston this week. Couldn't fly. Charlotte generously changed the plan and brought the kids down here to me."

Will pieced it together now. The spring break plan this year was to be a staycation to do touristy things with Ollie, who hadn't spent much time in Boston yet. One more example of how Charlotte kept the gears for their family life running smoothly. "I'd love to take you guys to the beach, but I may not go in; I couldn't find my swimming trunks at home."

Charlotte appeared from the bedroom. "They're here." She held up a small mesh packable with both his and her swimming suits in it.

Will followed her as she opened it and whispered to her, "So, you expected me?"

"Don't flatter yourself," Charlotte responded with a condescending look.

He followed her into their usual bedroom and raised a questioning eyebrow to her as he looked at the queen-sized bed, wondering how she could explain a different bedroom for him to Ollie and the kids. She threw her shoulders back in frustration before abruptly marching out of the room, spitting out the words, "You will stay on your side," between gritted teeth.

———— ⬦ ————

Over the next two days, Will kept up with the office in little snatches of time and texted Andrea to inquire about Chet. With both Will and Charlotte coaching Ollie through his Epley positional maneuvers, his vertigo was on the wane.

Beyond necessary social conversation, Will had not been able to get any focused time with Charlotte. The closest they had come to physical proximity was when Andy jumped into the wide gap between them to snuggle in bed one morning.

"Let's make a sandwich!"

When Charlotte was forced to turn toward him, Will was grateful Andy was still a cuddler, until he saw a tear roll down her cheek. He swallowed hard and got up quickly.

"Do you suppose Grandpa has pancake supplies in the kitchen?" he asked, leading his son away from the room and his own shame.

One night, they had barbecue on the patio and brought blankets and a chair for Ollie closer to the beach to watch the sunset. Will built a bonfire and Charlotte helped the kids assemble s'mores. As the faces of those he loved lit up with the leaping flames from the fire, Will teared up. By the time Will was Tish's age, his own mother was dead, after a miserable battle with breast cancer, and his dad wasn't far behind her, never himself after she was gone.

"Family story time!" Tish announced.

In the past, Will remembered groaning at such moments, but now he savored building memories with his family, so different from his family of origin. He recalled Charlotte's shock when she first learned Will had lost both his parents by the time he was nineteen.

"I can't imagine it. Growing up without my parents. I don't know how you coped."

Once they were serious about a life together, she did everything she could to make Will a part of her family, sharing her parents and her family norms with him, and using that blueprint as they started their own family.

"So, I've got a good one," Ollie said. "Have I ever shared with you kids how your dad asked for your mom's hand in marriage?"

"Ohh, no, Grandpa. Good one. Let's hear it!" Tish giggled and reached over her brother to poke her dad. "Is it romantic?"

Will stole a glance at his wife, whose beautiful face glowed in the firelight. He caught her eye and saw a slight smile threatening. "Let's hear Grandpa tell it."

"Well, your mom brought your dad to visit your grandma and me a couple of times, and we knew they were serious, but we didn't know your dad very well." Ollie took a sip of his bourbon. "Your dad, as you know, is a bright guy and it was pretty evident he was going places, that was for sure. One day, I got a call from him, saying, 'Oliver, will you and Sylvia be home tomorrow? I'd like to fly in to talk to you if I could.' Very formal like. I told him we didn't have any plans, and we'd be here. It was so odd that I was tempted to call your mom to find out what was going on, but your grandma, just smiled and said, 'Nope, it's a visit just between us. You will not call Charlotte.' But the appointed hour came and went. Fifteen minutes, then thirty. He was late." Ollie looked at Will. "Do you want to take the next part of the story?"

"Nope, you're doing good, Ollie," Will said, chuckling.

"So just about an hour late, we finally get a knock on the door. Your dad looked a bit rattled . . . no, actually, looked very rattled . . . more than I've ever seen your dad look." He chuckled lightly. "Kids, I wish you could have seen him. He was so nervous about blowing it with his potential in-laws!"

Tish couldn't contain herself. "So, what happened? Why was he so late?"

"He had the wrong address! He couldn't call Charlotte to get the right one and ruin the surprise, and he was too embarrassed to call us!"

"So, how did you figure it out, Dad?" Andy asked.

"Not telling." Will laughed. "The story is too good with the mystery intact!"

They all laughed, Ollie the loudest.

"Anyway, he was nervous as a cat by the time he got to our house, and once he finally got the words out, he didn't really relax until we gave him a hearty approval." Ollie's voice softened and took on a more serious tone. "Keeping your dad away from your mom would have been a travesty. They belong together. It was meant to be."

"Aww . . ." Tish got up from her position between her parents and smushed them together. "They do belong together, for sure."

Will took the invitation and leaned over to kiss his wife, but she turned her head and pulled away so that he just brushed her cheek.

"Is that the end of the story, Grandpa?" Andy asked.

"Yeah, I guess so. Well, except that because he was so late, he was going to miss his flight back, so he stayed the night. We ended up playing cards and talking like old friends by the end of his visit."

When the bonfire was out, Charlotte stood and hurried away toward the house, leaving Will to gather the gear on his own.

CHAPTER 13

▮▮▮▮▮▮▮▮▮▮▮▮▮▮▮▮▮▮▮▮

The next day, wild rain pounded the roof and wind forced the palm trees to nearly kiss the ground. Will stayed close to the kids and engaged with the family in board games, LEGO building with Andy, and a particularly competitive game of pool with his wife.

After he missed a fairly easy shot, Charlotte put her hands on her hips and said, "I think we both know who the real loser is here."

"Well, I'm committed to improving," he said carefully, then gestured for her to take her turn. He hoped she, too, was remembering their early dating life when Charlotte, in an effort she later confessed was designed to help him loosen up, took him to pubs with pool and cheap beer and showed him how to play a little. She wanted him to leave the pressures of academia and lab regimen to learn to be nimble and lose every once in a while. And he lost most of the time.

She took a turn and almost finished the game of eight-ball, prancing around the table and hitting ball after ball into the right pocket. "Watchya gonna do now, Mr. Franklin?" Their antics brought their children to the game room to watch.

He studied the table slowly for his audience and asked, "Andy, Tish, what should I do here?"

"Give up?" Andy offered. "Mom's got it, Dad."

"Hmmm." Will studied some more, then looked directly at Charlotte. "Your mom may have the game. I think you're right." He positioned himself to take the only shot available. "But give up? Never, no matter how many mistakes I've made."

Will took the shot, made it, but lost the game.

The kids yelled, "Yay Mom, way to go!" as Will crossed the floor to his wife and kids for high fives all around.

Will cast eager eyes at Charlotte and asked her, "Maybe we could figure out a spot for a pool table at home?"

"We'll see." Charlotte walked away and put her cue stick in the rack.

Later that afternoon, Amy called Will and launched in before he could get out a full hello.

"My father's not doing well at all, and Andrea isn't answering my calls."

"Slow down. Could you give me some context, please? I haven't been in contact with Andrea myself today and don't have the latest on Chet's condition. What's going on?"

"Nothing, that's the problem. He's still on life support and isn't making any progress." Her voice wobbled a bit.

"They were able to surgically seal off the aneurism in his brain though, right?"

"Yes, but they had to perform a follow-up craniotomy to help relieve increased intracranial pressure. Right now, part of his skull has been removed, and the pressure is unstable."

"Ohmygod. Have you been able to see him?"

"Yes, I've been a regular visitor. I'm still dodging Andrea at the hospital."

"Wow, this situation with Chet has got to be a low point for her."

"Yes, I'm aware of that, and am not heartless. Regardless, my dad needs someone to advocate for him during this nightmare, and Andrea is really almost a silent bystander."

Will couldn't challenge Amy. He didn't consider Andrea to be assertive in most situations, and it wasn't fair to expect she'd be a strong advocate for her husband right now. "So, what are you suggesting?"

"I can help here. I'm a nurse, and I can help navigate this on behalf of the family, for Dad."

"I agree it would be helpful. You've tried to reach Andrea?"

"Yes, many times, but she doesn't respond. Since she's the health-care agent for Dad, I can't insert myself into that role without her support. I need you to intervene. Can you talk to her and explain I mean no interference . . . I just want to support her?"

Will thought of how difficult her position was. She seemed like a self-assured woman who saw a way to help her dad, and a roadblock stood in her way. He didn't know if the roadblock would yield. Chet hadn't confided in him about past estrangements Amy had claimed were now bridged without Andrea in that loop. He did recall Chet loved Amy dearly and spoke of her early childhood years with fond memories of the boating club and Fenway Park. "Yes, I'll do what I can. I'll try right now."

"Thanks." He heard the relief in her voice. "And by the way, I finally remembered Dad mentioning you but couldn't place the name. He described you as an honorary son. You know he would appreciate your help now, right?"

A lump formed in Will's throat. "Yes, I do, Amy. I'll get back to you as soon as I can."

Will called Andrea immediately, and she answered on the first ring. "Will, Chet's not doing . . ." Her voice broke.

"Take your time. What's going on?"

"Nothing good. The surgery is over, but they had to remove part of his skull!" Her voice dropped. "Danny was in pieces after seeing him again yesterday. I'm kicking myself for allowing it."

"I'm sure it was tough for him, but I think it needed to happen. You did the right thing."

"We'll see. I need to stay strong so I can help Danny through this."

"Andrea, I got a call from Amy just now."

"And?" Andrea asked sharply.

"I think she may be able to offer some support to you, regarding Chet. As a nurse, she has a better medical understanding than we do, and she'd like to help. She said she's tried to reach you. She doesn't want to interfere. She wants to help."

Andrea was silent for so long, Will spoke again. "How does that sound to you?"

"I don't quite know how to think about it. You told me she and Chet had been in contact recently, but that's news to me. I'm not sure of her motive here."

"I can't get into your family dynamic, but it seems to me if she's telling you she and Chet have been in contact, then it would be worth hearing her out."

"It is complicated to decipher what the doctors are telling me—"

"Exactly, and I can't help you with that." He waited a moment. "What do you say? Give her a call?"

"Yes, I think I will." Andrea finally relented.

Will took a couple of deep breaths before his shoulders fell back into place. His heart raced, thinking about Chet's condition and his own neglect of Andrea over the past few days. *What kind of friend am I?* His face flushed, remembering how, just days ago, he wanted to go to Chet's hospital room and see the man for himself to see if there was any way he could make peace with Chet for whatever he thought Will had done. That possibility seemed out of reach now. He had let go of his fear of being fired but couldn't let go of the question mark of his last meeting with Chet. The combination of guilt for not having stayed closer to Andrea over the past few days, and the update on Chet's condition brought it all back in a flash.

That was before his marriage became his priority over his career, his reputation, and his relationship with Chet.

Ollie was in the kitchen when Will walked in to make himself a cup of tea. "I have a plan to hatch with you." He pulled Will in close. "The kids have been invited to movie and pizza night at the club with some friends."

"Yeah, okay," Will said. "Does Charlotte know?"

"Does Charlotte know what?" His wife appeared.

"You know how I try to make sure you and Charlotte can have a date night when you visit; tonight might be the night to do that." Ollie put his arms out to give his daughter a squeeze and directed his next comment to her. "Remember that new seafood place near Jensen Beach you wanted to try next time you came?"

"Yes, I do remember. Nice of you to think of that, Dad." She squeezed him back. "Does this have anything to do with the fact that tonight is your poker night, and you don't want to feel guilty leaving us on our own?" Charlotte teased.

"What do you say to date night with your wife, Will?" Ollie asked.

Even as Charlotte grimaced toward her husband, Will said, "Works for me." He offered a broad smile to both of them. "Thanks, Ollie. Can I take the car?"

Will did his best to put the news about Chet behind him, but he knew his emotions were close to the surface. Adrift as in a hurricane, Will was desperate to patch things up with Charlotte and go home to safety. Putting on the charm and starting off in the bar with a cocktail, he made several attempts to engage in chatter about the kids, how Ollie was doing and how the re-development effort in the area was coming along.

He was about to ask the server to take them to their table when Charlotte finally spoke in more than a syllable. "Will, stop. I'm out on this date night because Dad arranged it, and I didn't want to disappoint him. Things are not back to normal between us, so don't act as if they are."

It was a slap in the face, but at least she was talking. He breathed deeply and started over. "I know this wasn't your plan, but I was hoping we could use the time together to talk about what I can do to get us through this. Could we do that, please?"

Before she could respond, they were seated in an intimate nook with a view of the water, and the waiter took their order.

"We can talk. But right now, you need to listen. If you think coming down here to Florida makes everything all right, and we go back to normal . . . you couldn't be more wrong. Grand gestures will not make it right. I didn't expect you and didn't really want you here. I wanted time to think, on my own." Charlotte gazed out the window.

The waiter brought wine and poured them each a glass. Will pinched his knee in an effort to calm himself while he waited for her to finish.

"You have hurt me deeply. I don't know how we can get back to where we were. Not sure that is even possible. What I do know is that I am not ready to trust you." Charlotte's voice trembled. She cast her eyes down and took a sip of wine.

Will's temples pounded. "I couldn't stay away. I love you too much to have done that. I want you to know I won't do anything to jeopardize our relationship, our family, ever again. It will be a challenge for me to forgive myself for risking it." He quickly focused on the ceiling, blinking fast. "I will do everything in my power to regain your trust." He took her hand, "Charlotte, I would be so grateful if you would give me a chance to prove myself to you and seek your forgiveness."

He slowly pulled her hand to him and kissed it, while they both let their tears fall. Finally, Charlotte pulled away to dab her eyes.

"This week is a start, but we have a long way to go. You know that, right?" Charlotte took a breath.

He leaned in and kissed her lightly on the cheek. This time, mercifully, she didn't pull away. "I do, yes. Thank you for giving me a chance. I couldn't really get along without you, you know. This whole thing has sharpened my perspective on what you've meant to me over the years, the supportive love, advice, and counsel. It is all more than I ever dreamed of, and I have taken it for granted." He swallowed hard. "I promise I won't do that again. But, before we move forward, I owe it to you to tell you something else."

Charlotte straightened in her chair. "There's more?"

It poured out of him. Will told her about being summoned by Chet for a meeting at the boat club, and the message he delivered regarding Will's imminent dismissal. He described Chet's steely eyes, his unsteady gait as he rose, his empty glass of bourbon that may or may not have been the reason for his slurred speech.

Charlotte's eyes grew big. She stared at her husband with disbelief. "What? Why? Did he say why?"

Before Will could lose his nerve to take the biggest risk in his life, he answered her, the words seared in his memory forever, accessible to him only as exact repetition. "Chet said, 'Chasing tail is adolescent. And chasing tail when offered for a business trade is fatal. And when the product is a fraud, stupid and unforgivable.'"

CHAPTER 14

████████████████████

M uffled giggling through the closed bedroom door was
followed by urgent whispering. "Tish, c'mon!" Rousing,
Will opened an eye to bright sunlight just before Andy and
Tish exploded into the room. Andy ran ahead.

"Daddy, wake up! Mom says you've slept for twelve hours!"

Tish carefully offered him a mug of coffee. "Here, you
gotta get up. You and Grandpa are taking us to the Port St.
Lucie Botanical Gardens today. Mom's cooking Grandpa's
favorites to stock his freezer before we leave."

"Well, good morning to you, too." Will inched his way
to a sitting position and gratefully took the coffee while Andy
tousled his hair. "This is a serious case of bedhead, Dad!"

"Yeah, you'll definitely need to shower." Tish commanded.
"So, drink up and get moving, I really want to see the addi-
tions to the Orchid Room before we go home tomorrow."

"Tomorrow?"

"Yeah, Mom got us all on a flight together in the morning."

Hearing the phrase "flight together" brought such relief
that Will smiled broadly, the memory of last night now in
focus. "Give me fifteen minutes, and I'll be ready to go."

As he showered, Will recalled the particulars of Charlotte's
response to his confession about Chet planning to fire him.

She seemed as baffled as he had been at the news. She asked him lots of questions about Chet's state of mind that day, their most recent interactions, and what they had been working on together currently.

He told her everything he had thought of to try to determine if Chet had done anything concrete to move forward on his plan to fire him.

"You checked all of his devices, both incoming and outgoing, right?"

Will was thrilled to have Charlotte's keen mind working on his behalf to assess the news that his job was at risk. He almost forgot he had also just asked his wife to forgive him for the folly of his fling.

"How did Chet know about your affair?" she asked. Only the narrowing of her eyes hinted at the pain it caused. "If he knew, others may also know. Have you thought of all that?"

Will fought off his shame as he had to explain to his wife. "I've been racking my brain and don't know how he could. We never met in public other than at a business lunch or event. Both times we met at a hotel, in New York and Boston. Nothing was under my name."

Charlotte's eyebrows shot up, and she shook her head before responding to him. "There are no secrets. You are a fool to think so. This is bigger than your fling. It's time to go home and figure it out."

Will couldn't leave it. "Together, right?"

"For now." Her voice grew softer. "You know you have to regain my trust, and I don't know yet how this story ends."

Her answer was all he had a right to expect. It was enough to allow his depleted body and soul to maintain an upright posture until he got back to Ollie's and his side of the bed, where he fell asleep immediately.

Five days of newspapers scattered across the front entry greeted their return to the Belmont house. At least he had remembered to put the garbage out. Charlotte went about getting their household routine organized as if he had not shaken their world with his behavior. She had given him back a modicum of normalcy, and his path forward. He could not afford to be paralyzed by the crisis in his marriage. He needed to sort out the mystery behind Chet's threat. As in the past, Charlotte's ability to see the big picture and point out the land mines in his way was clear. They both needed to see how this story ended in order to find their way back to each other.

Since it was Sunday afternoon, he caught up on work in his home office. He breathed in the essence of home. Charlotte's touch was all around him. A believer in comfort as well as style in furnishings, she knew him so well, she had gotten this room exactly right. He had always loved it. Leather wing chairs and couch, huge ottoman, side tables, one entire wall of bookshelves and interesting items from their years abroad, interspersed with family pictures and memorabilia. Awards for scientific accomplishments subtly displayed among them.

He pulled Chet's phone and computer out of their case to review any communication activity he had missed over the past few days away. Two weeks out from Chet's stroke, he didn't expect much personal traffic. Emails didn't provide anything new. He picked up the phone to check any activity. A missed call from Robin Warren. The name sounded familiar. He studied his notes. There was an earlier call from her, but no email. He added her name to his tomorrow list, along with Clark and Larry.

After dinner, Will helped Charlotte clean up and brought her up to date on Chet's serious complications, his call from Amy, and how Amy and Andrea were still not in contact.

"That's a lot for Andrea to take in. I plan to visit her early this week to check on what they need." Charlotte added, "You know, when I visited Andrea before the Florida trip, I did ask her about Chet's daughter, if she had been in touch at all. And she was uncharacteristically curt when she answered, 'Why do you ask?' When I explained since Chet was her dad, she might care about his well-being,' she snipped back with. 'That's news to me. She's not been in our lives for years.' Clearly there's a volatile family dynamic at work here. We should be careful."

"Yes, for sure." Will focused on his wife's use of "we." He said, "I'll be getting a condition report on Chet tomorrow and let you know before you make your plan to visit Andrea."

———⟡———

Merilee saw him get off the elevator and removed her headphones to stand up and greet him at the office the next morning.

"Hey boss, welcome back. I'm so glad you were able to join the family in Port St. Lucie. You've had a lot to deal with lately. How was it?"

"So good. It's amazing what a few days away can do for one's well-being. Thanks for asking." Charlotte had given Will new grounding and he was ready for whatever came next.

"I caught up as much as I could last night, but let's pull the Exec Team together late morning for a debrief on the hacking situation. Will you ask Larry to drop by my office before that?"

When Larry arrived, Will asked him for an update on the hacking recovery beyond BioteKem. He knew Larry would be a catchall for industry gossip on how the insiders now thought about the payout and any potential for future plans to combine forces and not be picked off.

"Pretty hush-hush, generally. Nobody wants to rock the boat." Larry stretched his long frame out and crossed a leg over his knee. "Chickens, all of them. I think time will do the trick. This last one is still too fresh. In another month or so, we should make another pitch to pull together." He uncrossed his leg. "What's the news on Chet? Is he really in bad shape? That's what I keep hearing."

Larry's prompt led Will right where he wanted to go. "He's not good. I'm about to get a condition report this morning, and we'll have to get something out to folks before long. How far has the rumor spread?" Will knew not to ask Larry to reveal his sources.

"Not far. But it would be helpful to get some facts out, so folks don't go crazy with conjecture."

"Anybody getting particularly anxious or ready to jump on an opportunity to create chaos for us during a potential transition?" Will asked.

Prompted by Charlotte to think more strategically, he realized he had not considered jealousy from among his team or board as a possible motive for pulling him down. This gave him new energy to investigate a whole new cadre of people from a different direction, those who may have poisoned Chet against him. Before he canvassed all of them, he wanted to see if Larry had any intelligence to share.

"You know human nature. Self-interest abounds. However, I don't see anyone jockeying to knock you off as successor CEO. That would be a foolish move."

Will smiled. "Thanks."

Larry got up to leave. "By the way, Merilee gave me that packet of papers that you got from Andrea. I haven't taken a look at it yet. Is it a priority?"

"No, not at all, just when you get a chance. I assume it's something to do with the Foundation."

After Larry left, Will pulled up the board list on his computer and printed it out so he could make hand notes. He scanned the list with an eye toward any recent interaction he had with each of them and how comfortable he was with their support for him. While he had been heir apparent since they recruited him two years ago, there was no announcement in the offing about a succession timetable, as far as he knew. Perhaps Chet had been doing that secretly before his stroke.

It occurred to him that although corporate communications and emails went out almost daily about what was happening, he had not personally talked to all of the board members in the past two weeks. Beyond "attaboy" messages from a few of them, he assumed each of them was spending time with their primary jobs. All were in leadership roles in their own companies, and some were dealing with cyberattack response, just like he was at BioteKem. Merilee had let them all know immediately about Chet's hospitalization.

Maybe individual conversations were in order, just as a well-being check. It might reveal any guilt or worry. *How would betrayal reveal itself?*

CHAPTER 15

He thought about asking Merilee to arrange calls to each board member but decided he would prefer making the unexpected calls personally in order to enhance the impact. He wanted to surprise them. He expected to start making calls that afternoon, curious about how many he would get to without having to leave a callback request. Just the act of taking his call immediately would tell him something.

He called Clark for a condition report on Chet. He didn't want to get between Amy and Andrea today until he knew what was going on.

"Not at all good. I'm sorry, but I think there is only one way this ends."

"Can't they do anything else?"

"I think they've done everything they can do. They can't manage the intracranial pressure, and his organs are failing. It's really just a matter of time. The family will need to pull together to make a tough decision."

Will thanked Clark and rang off, his mind crowded with conflicting thoughts. He had motivation to let Chet die— more than he could admit to anyone—yet his emotions took him on a roller-coaster ride of gratitude for everything Chet had done for him and been for him in the years Chet had mentored him. He was a father figure to emulate. Now he had to work hard to block the resentment that was not far below the surface for the mysterious motive that would lead Chet to fire him.

He called Charlotte to pass on the sad news. Together they determined Charlotte should either make a visit in the next day or wait, as a condolence visit may be in the offing.

"I'll call her now," Charlotte said.

He started his board calls with Carter MacNamara, an old friend of Chet's who ran a life sciences company and had made a fortune advising companies on drug development. If anyone was aware of Chet's animosity, Will guessed it would be him. Carter took his call.

"Is everything okay with Chet?" Carter sounded worried.

"He's facing some complications, so it's a very dangerous situation."

"How's Andrea?"

"Hanging in there. It's a terrible time for them."

"Unbelievable. Who would have expected . . ." Carter's voice was strained. "I really feel so bad for Chet and his family."

"I know. It's terrible. I'm staying close to the family and will keep you informed." Will cleared his voice. "Right now, Carter, I need some feedback. Are you getting what you need from BioteKem from a communications perspective? Are we keeping you informed of the business issues going through the cyberattack? I'm reaching out to each board member just to assure all of you that I'm fully engaged with doing what needs to be done. I'd appreciate your honest appraisal of how I'm doing specifically. Any issues with my performance?"

"Are you kidding?" Carter said. "You haven't missed a beat since this thing started. You've got a full vote of confidence from me. Have you got doubts about your support?"

"No, not at all, it's just such a strange time, and with Chet out for now . . ." Will tried to prevent a wobble from creeping into his voice but couldn't. "I wanted to be sure the board was with me."

"Well, I'm with you. It's a helluva thing how you're helping out with Chet's family. If you get a whiff of anything from any other members, I want you to let me know."

He got three more calls in, left two messages, and had a short but supportive conversation with Robert Hawkiss, a long-time board member who Chet told him was on the search committee when they recruited him in. He expected Hawkiss to be supportive, and he was. He dared ask, "So, had you been in recent contact with Chet about his own plans?"

"Not too recent. A month or so ago, maybe."

Will could visualize the tall, elegant gentleman folding his long legs and leaning back in his chair to consider the question carefully.

"January, I'm thinking?" He paused, then started up again, slowly. "Said he was getting close to a decision, had some family issues he wanted to address first. Not sure what that meant. He didn't go into it."

Will repeated his request for an honest appraisal of his own performance.

"As far as I'm concerned, Will, we're ready with you in the wings for whatever or whenever Chet's successor needs to be named."

He decided to quit for now, somewhat comforted by the first responses, and took time to scroll through Chet's devices for anything new. Only one new call from Robin Warren. This time she left a message.

"Mr. Sutherland. We're getting close now. It's time for a quote if you are going to make one. Call me."

Will was in a quandary about how to handle Robin Warren. Calling her back to explain the situation with Chet was wrong for at least two reasons. First, if she was in Chet's close circle, she would know about his current situation. If she wasn't, he shouldn't be the one to bring this stranger into an intimate circle of friends. Second, he had no idea what type of request she was making and didn't want to take the time to get sidelined on something that wasn't important. It sounded like she could be asking for an industry opinion on a new device or therapy for an article someone was writing. There would be no quote forthcoming, so it was not relevant.

He searched for her on LinkedIn, but there were too many Robin Warrens to chase down, so left it. While on LinkedIn, he moved to Bella's profile. He hadn't heard anything from her and didn't want to.

He clicked on Bella's picture. She wore a white lab coat over her signature black. Her thick glasses hid her eyes, dangling earrings floating to her collar. It could be recent. He scanned her profile, realizing he knew little about her beyond her reputation as a rising star. That made him feel worse. As he remembered, she was interested in his own career track, having been an academic who moved into the business side of biotech, and she wanted to learn about the how of it.

She had come on strong at the Philadelphia meeting. He could tell himself she lured him into a private room and came on to him, practically arranging their first night together in five minutes of steamy flirtation. He could have redirected their interaction into something that would have become a genuine mentorship arrangement. He should have been what his brand said he was—the mature established biotech leader willing to help young talent find their way. He claimed that was an interest of his when he spoke at industry functions. Had he taken advantage of her? As a woman trying to make it in biotech, did she think this is what it took?

Now, he carefully read her profile, learning details about her he hadn't known. Stanford PhD, yes. But there was lots of new stuff, too, including research with Jens Larsen at UCLA and a stint in Silicon Valley at a start-up, which developed and commercialized products with direct sales of over $1 billion, acquired by Cutter & Barrow for $460 million. He wondered how much cash she walked away with to start her new venture. He remembered the line from their first meeting.

"I'm about to change the world with a new way to control diabetes."

It seemed to shout out to him.

The company had a PO Box in Silicon Valley. Nothing on the East Coast that he saw on the profile. He was embarrassed he didn't even know where she lived. His interest in her was a fun distraction from the cushioned life he led, something he thought he deserved now that he was at the top of his field, waiting to be named to his dream job. He admitted to himself there was a physical attraction to Bella, but every bit as tempting was the sense of novelty and renewal this fling brought to him. Bella represented all of the girls he never had the opportunity to date when he was a young, naive nerd, fearful of rejection, when he never had the nerve to ask. Her passion for the discovery side of research reminded him of himself when he was still in the lab.

He marveled at how selfish he had been. Through the lens of life-and-death issues of the last weeks, not only did he feel a new understanding of priorities, but deeply ashamed of his behavior. Was his own life of privilege so boring he had to create some drama?

His current work was the most meaningful he had been engaged in for a long time. It was appealing to lead his company and his business associates into a grand-scale effort to keep things moving to patients during the cybersecurity disruption and not just focus on making money. It reminded him of his rewarding days in the lab when he was so other-focused. Since those early years, selfless had been hard to do. It got lost in the pursuit of deals and acquisitions of promising therapies to bring to market. There was a large societal good that came of the work his company did, what he did to bring solutions to market, to scale up for populations of patients that needed these therapies. But the satisfaction was further removed now.

It was time to reassess his priorities. He needed to reconnect with Charlotte again on their future. He tried to remember the last time they had a serious talk about their lives. Maybe when they came back from Barcelona for this job? Their challenge then was to figure out how to evaluate the opportunity before them. What it meant for their family and their future. It had taken them weeks to consider all of the ramifications. Charlotte, so instrumental in helping him see his strengths, was the first to see this as the steppingstone it was, but she held her enthusiasm until he got there. He was always a bit slower than she was. He missed her.

CHAPTER 16

"**D**r. Franklin?" Merilee had put a call through to Will.
"Yes, Pam, what's up?" It was Pam Shields from the
BioteKem communications staff.

"I wanted to alert you to a piece in today's BiotechNews
online feed. There's a mention of BioteKem, and I thought
you should see it. I'm sending you the link now. Let me know
if you want me to respond in any way."

"Okay, thanks. Is this one of the big ones for circulation?"
He didn't recognize the name. There were so many news
outlets now, it was hard to keep up. Many of them were
just re-circulating what the more prominent outlets reported.

"Not one of the big ones, no, but I'm watching to see if
this gets picked up anywhere else."

"I'll open it in a couple of minutes. Thanks." He wondered
why she hadn't kicked it up to her boss, then remembered
she was new in this role and didn't know how many rumors
and miscommunications were struck down every day. Biotech
was like a small town getting bigger all the time, and lots of
positioning happened by starting a game of telephone.

The headline, "Possible SEC Investigation May Dim
Rising Star's Prospects" hooked him, and the glamour shot
felled him. Bella Davis. Smoky eyes, flawless face contoured

with makeup, and hair slicked back, showcasing her perfect bone structure, and highlighting her direct gaze. Her only recognizable feature was dangling silver earrings, this time free-falling to a bare neck.

His head pounded as he forced his gaze from the photo to the article.

"An anonymous source has reported that Bella Davis, the young Stanford PhD, fresh from a sale of a previous start-up to Cutter & Barrow for $460 million, is now the CEO of a new venture that is the likely subject of an SEC investigation," the story began, followed by filler about Bella he had just yesterday read on LinkedIn. A new tidbit followed.

"Davis has been working the scientific meeting circuit to pitch her new company, Met-Med, a privately held, commercially oriented biotech company. Estimated to have approximately $10 M of capital backing, the company was said to be focused on metabolic medicine and currently in proof-of-concept testing for life-changing diabetes treatment.

"The source reported, 'Davis is on the East Coast meeting with investors for an equity call' and inferred the activity had prompted the interest of the SEC. BioteKem was the only biotech company mentioned by the source as a company of potential interest in a joint venture or other alliance. We were not able to reach anyone at BioteKem to confirm or deny any association with Ms. Davis."

Will read the article three times, always missing something until he realized he was missing what was not there—any clue to this puzzle.

He took a couple of deep breaths to calm down. SEC investigations were a big deal. Biotech may look like an open horizon and act like the Wild West on occasion, but nobody wanted trouble with the SEC.

What had Bella gotten herself into? Was she a victim here, or the bad girl that just got caught?

The picture combined with the headline could be taken as an effort to take this beautiful young upstart down, a comeuppance for aiming too high. If it was a false rumor to trip her up, why would anyone want to do that? Jealousy, a deal gone bad, misogyny gone crazy? He quickly searched online to confirm his own knowledge of the types of trouble that could lead to an SEC investigation.

- Misrepresentation or omission of important information about securities
- Manipulation of the market prices of securities
- Stealing customers' funds or securities
- Violating broker-dealers' responsibility to treat customers fairly
- Insider trading (violating a trust relationship by trading on material, nonpublic information about a security)
- Selling unregistered securities

The more he thought about her predicament, he was puzzled he was not furious at her and the mention of BioteKem. He had immediately wanted to take her side. He then realized his first emotion of empathy for her must have originated in how he identified with her for being wrongly judged by Chet. Accused of an SEC violation with no champion to defend her. Just like Will had been. Chet hurling accusations at Will for fraudulent business activity without giving him any explanation or opportunity to defend himself. It led Will to entertain the possibility he had been set up. Was it possible both Bella and Will had been set up? Someone trying to take Bella down by spreading a false rumor about her company? Could Chet have been an unknowing party to deception also? If only he could talk to Chet.

He bolted from his chair to stretch his coiled body. He walked around his office and glanced out at the harbor, letting his mind wander until it found the next mile marker. He stopped cold. *Can there be a link here?* With a flush of regret, he thought back to his eager willingness to succumb to Bella's charms, thinking little about consequences to his personal life, but never worrying about his professional life.

Chet and the SEC. Could Chet have been drawn to a false conclusion during an interview process? What if Chet had been interviewed in regard to Bella's company as part of its investigation and they floated the idea that BioteKem—Will—was interested in an investment or partnership opportunity? Chet would have been furious. He had given Will wide berth to do what was best in all areas of the company, more so now that Chet himself was in the exit lane. It wasn't unreasonable to think a start-up might approach BioteKem seeking an anchor interest in their future. But, unreasonable in Chet's eyes would be that Will would not have talked to him about any such approach. Keeping his safe perch as BioteKem Board Chair, the all-knowing, not-to-be blindsided, board chair emeritus was paramount in his thinking—and in his standing in the biotech world. Any potential SEC investigation tied remotely to BioteKem would besmirch his legacy. Chet wouldn't allow that to happen.

He read the line about BioteKem again. "We were not able to reach anyone at BioteKem to confirm or deny any association with Ms. Davis." This time he noticed the byline.

Robin Warren. The name in Chet's phone and email records that he hadn't recognized. He pulled out Chet's phone to replay her voice mail.

"Mr. Sutherland. We're getting close now. It's time for a quote if you are going to make one. Call me."

Was Robin Warren trying to get a quote from Chet regarding any BioteKem interest in Bella's company? She wrote this article, and it fit she would keep trying to get a quote from Chet. It also fit she wouldn't know he had been hospitalized after a stroke. *Looks like she got tired of waiting.*

Will pushed his chair from his desk abruptly. He needed to put distance between himself and Chet's phone. He stood to walk the room, silently managing his frustration. He remembered his commitment to reprioritize, with family being on the top of the list. He wanted to spend more time cogitating on what all of this SEC business meant, but instead, he forced himself to drive home.

Later that evening, Will asked Charlotte how her visit with Andrea had gone.

"It was hard, but I'm so happy I called her. She eagerly accepted my offer of grocery shopping, so I went straight from the grocery store and had the kids with me. I picked up pizza. Tish and Danny seemed to hit it off. The distraction helped, I think, and Andy liked hanging out with the big kids. We stayed quite a while. Andrea wanted to talk."

"Anything new?"

He noticed Charlotte squirm before she answered. "Yes. Actually, I'm not sure what it means, but it was curious what she shared with me."

Will joined her at the kitchen island and grabbed a few towels from the laundry basket to help fold. "More about her suspicions about Chet?" He wanted to keep her talking. Any intimacy he could find with her was a bonus, even if the topic of possible adultery would not have been his choice.

Charlotte bit her lip and took some time as if to decide whether she would tell him. "I'm not sure she would want me to share this with you." She scanned his face and then busied herself with folding. "But I think it's important for us to consider what it means, given Chet's threat to your job."

Will gave her another minute. "What was it? Did she know about that?"

"No, definitely not. She wouldn't have told me what she did if she thought Chet was about to fire you." Charlotte now committed to telling him what she learned. "I did ask her about whether she had any more reason to believe Chet was involved with someone else. She told me she didn't. But when I asked her whether she had any new ideas about what was distracting him, she wanted to get my opinion."

Charlotte took a breath and continued. "It seems Chet was having second thoughts about retirement. He wasn't sure he was ready to hang it up. Evidently, he didn't want to feel that old."

Will's mouth gaped open. *Where is this coming from? I had no idea.*

"There's more. She said he was very excited about something new he was working on, something that would change BioteKem's strategic path and blow everyone's mind."

"Did she know what that something new was?" Will had stopped folding and could barely take a breath.

"No, said it was a secret. But it was big."

"Big and he couldn't share it with me?" Will stood up and ran his hand through his hair. "I thought I knew this man, but this is getting crazy. What was going on with him?" He walked the length of the kitchen before he added. "So, what advice did she ask for then?"

"Well, it wasn't advice exactly. I think she wanted reassurance from me about how she had responded to his plan to postpone retirement. She told me she thought it sounded a bit like a midlife crisis—his having second thoughts about retirement and maybe worried about their age difference becoming more of an issue if he retired and hung around the house more.

Charlotte raised an eyebrow. "She evidently told him she wanted him to go forward with his plans. She wanted to spend more time with him, travel with him, etc."

"And what did you say?"

"I thought he deserved a great retirement, and it was natural for somebody as powerful as Chet to have some qualms about moving into a new chapter. I reassured her."

"And what about the big secret. Did she ask you for advice about that?"

Charlotte stood to wrangle a larger bath sheet on the island surface. "No, but she did ask me whether Chet had told you about any possible delay to his retirement or about this new big thing. I told her that as far as I knew, he had not shared with you any retirement doubts, but given how much you respected him, you would probably be happy in that circumstance. I also told her it seemed odd Chet would not have shared news of something big going on for BioteKem."

"Good. What did she say then?"

"She was tearful and quiet for a while. Finally, she said she thought Chet's behavior was becoming more erratic and that all of what was happening, the possible affair, the retirement worry, and this big secret deal—she thought it was all part of whatever was wrong with him."

"Wrong with him, as in medically?"

"She didn't continue really, but I got the impression she believes there was something happening with Chet—that he was really not himself." Charlotte shrugged and took a minute to put the last folded towel in the basket before she answered. "She couldn't explain it, and frankly, I couldn't probe. It seemed too hurtful to her. She's barely coping as it is."

"Of course, you couldn't," Will said softly. "Andrea needed a friend today, and I'm glad you were there for her." He patted her shoulder. "It must be hell for her knowing she can't communicate with him now, left with her confusion about what was going on in his mind, and whether she could have helped him at all. I don't envy her the position she's in." Will realized he and Andrea had a common experience—not knowing what Chet had on his mind and left hanging in doubt.

"What do you make of it all?" Charlotte asked. "You said he was acting strange when you saw him the afternoon before his stroke. Do you think there was something medically wrong?"

"I don't know. Something else strange happened today that adds to the mystery. Are you up for another piece of the puzzle?" Will watched her body language. He didn't want to push her but could really use her insight. "I'll totally understand if you want to say no."

She stood up, laundry basket of folded towels resting on her hip. "Yes, after that odd conversation with Andrea, I'd really like to hear what else is going on. For everyone's sake."

"Good." Will took the laundry basket from her and started walking toward the stairs. "Follow me."

CHAPTER 17

W ill started by playing the voice mail from Robin Warren to Chet requesting a quote from him and telling Charlotte he hadn't responded to the request because he had never heard her name before, and she hadn't identified what type of quote she needed and why. Then he pulled up the Biotech News article online and turned the monitor so Charlotte could see it.

Too late. He remembered the photo of Bella as the centerpiece of the article. He watched Charlotte's face closely as he grew queasy. He saw her brow tighten, and then her eyes dart to the article itself.

When she finished reading, she angled the monitor back toward his chair. "I didn't know she was so beautiful," she said lightly. "Quite the brand she's building for herself."

"Charlotte, I'm sorry. It was insensitive of me to—"

"You told me the two of you never spoke business. She didn't ask you to champion a deal with BioteKem? Not even when you were 'mentoring' her in NYC?" Charlotte snipped.

"We never discussed her business dealings, and she never asked for anything from BioteKem." Will's voice was gentle. "I knew she was pitching to investors, that's all."

He flushed just thinking back.

Bella had sent him a few texts leading up to the Boston trip. It was clear her idea of a mentor/mentee relationship was not the traditional concept. He immediately deleted some of the more suggestive "Hoping you can show me some new tricks. Getting hot thinking about seeing you." He chalked it up to a younger generation thing, when he should have been the adult and gently ended it. Instead, by the time they met up for drinks at her hotel, he knew what would happen next. Science was not a topic of conversation.

Two weeks later, they had met up in New York City. She happened to be in town when he was there on business, and she came to him. Just one night. Nothing more than a hookup. Although, this time she asked him to tell her the full story about his career from when he was a young research associate through his departure from academia and to describe his career track once he jumped to biotech. Now, he remembered how he carefully left Charlotte's role out of the story, even though she was the architect of his move from academia. Charlotte was the one who saw in him the leadership and people skills that could be put to better use for the world if he embraced his business side. Charlotte saw in him a natural entrepreneur who could help bring life-saving therapies to people. Although his wedding ring was always in plain sight, he never once talked about his family with Bella. Those worlds were totally separate.

Bella flattered him with questions. "How did you go about gaining credibility to land your first job? Who were your important mentors along the way?"

She had seemed fascinated with his personal story. By the end of that second meeting in NYC, Will asked her what she wanted from him as a mentor. Almost twenty years older, he should have been wiser and was beginning to feel guilty that he wasn't doing anything to help her career. He still had not known much about her product line, and the business plan for launching it.

When he asked her to tell him about what progress she was making and what she needed, she told him the equity call was going well and mentioned the names of angel investors well known in biotech.

The plan was to spell out more detail for him when they were together at the Annual Global Healthcare Summit. This time, she would have her own room and be there for her own business to meet with a potential investor, this time an Italian in the country for the conference. She couldn't be in town early enough for Will's talk or the panel presentation. They had agreed any interaction at the conference would be at arms-length and had giggled thinking about the play-acting they would need to do in any chance meeting.

Then, everything fell apart.

Charlotte interrupted his thoughts. "So, when you connect the dots, are you assuming Chet thought you were involved in some way?"

"I don't know what to make of it. What I do know is that I wasn't involved in anything that would be of interest to the SEC. I don't know what Chet may have thought of me . . . or what Bella may be involved in. I'm in the dark." Will spoke from the heart, worried that—to the wife he betrayed and the world—it may not look like he was innocent of shady dealings.

"Listen to me. As I said the other day, this whole thing is even bigger than your fling." Charlotte cast her eyes to the ceiling, her voice getting louder as she continued, "and we still don't know how this story ends. It's getting murkier. You need to follow the source of the story. If this Robin Warren was waiting for a quote from Chet for the article, then she must have an idea who the anonymous source of the possible SEC investigation was. Wouldn't she also possibly know the name of the SEC investigator who may have interviewed Chet?"

Charlotte didn't disappoint. He knew he deserved nothing from her, and then she came up with a timely insight. Will pulled his torso from its slump, the corners of his mouth lifting slightly into a loving smile. "My God, yes! Charlotte, yes. Robin Warren may know. You're absolutely right."

"Of course, I am. And you're welcome."

———————⬦———————

During the night, Will had a recurring dream that he was in Chet's hospital room. This time he was able to recall the details the next morning. Alone with a body more like Darth Vader than Chet Sutherland, he had edged to the bed and tried to find one of Chet's hands to hold. Chet was so connected to tubes and beeping equipment he dared not touch him. Instead, he told his friend and mentor all about the cyberattack and how they were responding to it. He told him about Danny and Andrea, and how he had talked to Amy a few times and liked her. A nurse came in to fiddle with the equipment, but Will kept talking. Finally, Will put his face as close as he could to Chet's ear and said, "Tell me why, Chet. Why do you want to fire me? I won't be mad. I just need to find peace."

Will strained to see some sort of sign, an answer, a change in the beep tones, anything that would signal Chet had heard him. He considered how easy it would be for him to turn off one of these machines, pinch off the breathing tube . . . end what had become of Chet's life.

Then, suddenly, while he waited, Chet grew agitated, his body contorting as the beeping sounds changed to alerts. Lights blinked at the doorway, and he heard footsteps from the corridor coming into the room.

Will woke up gasping for air, afraid for the one long agonizing moment before he registered his familiar surroundings that he had taken an action which would end any hope to get an answer.

Still shaken the next morning, he chose to call Amy rather than Andrea. She answered on the second ring.

"Will, I'm glad you called. You can help."

"I'm always happy to help. What's happening."

"Lots. I guess I need to bring you up to speed." She slowed down a bit. "First, I should thank you for smoothing the path for me to get to Andrea. It worked." She seemed to choose her words carefully. "In fact, it worked so well, we've spent hours talking about the past—what happened between my father and me to cause the rift, and how he and I were able to patch it up."

"I'm glad to hear that. Has it helped?"

"Yes, yes it has helped. I believe she understands more about her husband, and while she wishes she had known it before, she's happy we are working it through now . . ."

"But?"

"Well, it all may be too late and irrelevant at this point." Her wistfulness now turned to business.

"Tell me."

"Dad's organs are failing. It's unlikely he'll be able to come back. His strength has failed him."

"I'm so sorry. Does Andrea know this and accept this?"

"Not yet. That's how you can help. I've scheduled a family conference with the doctor for late today. Andrea is happy to have me be a part of this. I'd like to have you on the call."

"I'm not family."

"No, but my dad considered you family, and Andrea really counts on you. Think about how you've been taking care of things for her and Danny." Amy lowered her voice a little. "Family helps out when it gets tough. I need your help to support Andrea through this. Will you help me . . . help us?"

Will didn't think she would accept "no" for an answer. The best he could counter with was, "If Andrea wants me on the call, I'll be on the call."

Will called Andrea to be sure. He didn't want to get between them at such a crucial time. "Yes, I'd really like your help. Amy's been great, but I do trust your judgment. If you could make the time, I'd be grateful."

He focused on the Chet who trusted him and not the Chet who was about to fire him or had some new big thing for BioteKem that he was keeping a secret. Clearly, it was that Will who Andrea had turned to the night she needed help. There was no way he could turn down this request for help now. He choked down the irony of a situation that put him on the call with the doctor to help decide how long they should take heroic measures to keep Chet alive, the Chet who had turned against him.

Amy texted directions for Will to add an app to his phone or computer for the video appointment with the doctor for 3:30 that afternoon. Will did so. Then he pulled Robin Warren's number up from Chet's phone and punched it in. Her crisp voice mail asked him to leave a brief message. He felt sure using Chet's name would get him a quick return response.

Two hours later, her call came in. He excused himself from his team meeting and took the call.

"Hello, this is Will Franklin."

"Yes, good morning Mr. Franklin. This is Robin Warren returning your call."

"Good. Thanks, Ms. Warren." Will cleared his throat and mentally got into character as an unknowing party attempting to learn more without giving much. "You left a voice message for Chet Sutherland a week or two ago, and I'm following up."

"Yes, I did." She responded slowly.

"Can you tell me why you were calling Mr. Sutherland?"

"Can you tell me why you're asking?"

"Yes, I've been asked to connect with people who had been in contact with Mr. Sutherland to see if there are matters pending that need to be tended to."

"Okay . . ." Robin sounded exasperated now. "Why is it that Mr. Sutherland can't respond himself?"

The moment of truth had arrived. Will had to give a little. "I'm afraid Mr. Sutherland has suffered a stroke and is in the hospital."

"Oh, I'm sorry to hear that. I had no idea." Her surprise sounded genuine.

"Yes, it was sudden, and now you may understand why we'd like to determine if there is anything that needs addressing. Mr. Sutherland is a high-profile person in the biotherapy space, and we'd like to make sure there is nothing that he would feel has been dropped due to his untimely illness. Is there?" Will heard some tapping and echo in the background. He assumed she was researching him online and changing her phone to speaker mode.

"Are you Will Franklin from BioteKem, then?"

"Yes, I am. But it was Mrs. Sutherland who asked me to follow-up. I have no idea if you called him on a personal basis or for business reasons."

"I see. I appreciate that you took the time to call me back. Not everyone would. I'm a freelance reporter. I was working on an article that had a tangential mention of BioteKem and wanted a quote from Mr. Sutherland, if possible."

"I see. Has the article been published? Would I have seen it?" Will turned now to controlling the flow of information.

"Not unless you read online BioTechNews." Robin sounded sheepish. "It's just one of many online outlets. Circulation is still building."

"I'm not aware of it, I'm afraid. What was the nature of the article?"

"Well, it had the makings of a scandal hook. A possible

SEC investigation with a newcomer young woman who's been making waves. I thought it would get a bigger footprint than it did. Uhh, sorry to ramble." He could almost see Robin sitting straighter in her chair to respond. "Because my source mentioned BioteKem as a potential buyer for the company, I was hoping to get a confirmation or denial of that piece."

"Mr. Sutherland never did confirm or deny, then?"

"Uh, no, I never even talked to him."

"Can you tell me who gave you his name?"

"My source."

"Was the source connected to the possible SEC investigation?"

"It was an anonymous tip. Sorry."

"Of course, I understand and appreciate your professionalism. I wonder, though, if your source is truly interested in BioteKem's business." He cleared his throat. "You could direct her or him to me."

"Yeah, that makes sense." Robin sounded thoughtful. "I mean, I don't think there's anything more to the story. I'll let her know."

"Thank you for your time."

All Will knew by the time he hung up was that the source was a "she." He decided it was time to bring in his general counsel, Larry, to dig into the SEC investigation possibilities. He went back to the website with the article and uploaded it to an email.

"Check this out, please."

He kept it brief to avoid arousing suspicion of any ulterior motive Will might have. Just a routine follow-up. No drama. Nothing personal.

The video call started promptly at 3:30 p.m. The shaky positioning of Andrea's tablet on her lap told the story of a woman barely hanging on. Despite the subject matter ahead, Will was transfixed by his first view of Chet's daughter. Maybe fifty years old, with a topknot of dark hair laced by silver strands, and deep-set, blue-gray eyes. The resemblance to her father caused his heart to skip a beat. Her confidence and warmth seemed to ooze from the screen, which showed a wall of abstract art over her head and shoulders.

Amy took the lead with introductions, explaining Will to the doctor as, "a family friend and trusted colleague of my father's." Will choked down his impostor syndrome and quietly said hello. Andrea looked fatigued, but added, "Thanks, Will, for being on the call with us. Chet would appreciate it."

They listened to the doctor summarize the course of Chet's illness over the course of the twenty days since his stroke, which followed conventional treatment and necessitated surgical intervention.

"While the surgical procedure to clip the bleed in his brain was not successful, he was able to tolerate the unfortunate complications for a period of time. But, at this point, we think his body is losing the battle."

Amy asked, "Dr. Burch, can you tell us if we have other treatments left to try?"

"As you know, hemorrhagic stroke is a high-risk situation. In Mr. Sutherland's case, the treatment indicated by his symptoms was to relieve the intracranial pressure caused by the aneurysm in his brain. As this treatment of choice was not successful, the body has now begun to shut down."

Andrea's body seemed to shrink into itself; she wiped a tear from her eye. "What do you mean, shut down?"

"The ventilator has kept his lungs functioning, but his organs are failing, and I'm afraid there is nothing more that can be done."

They talked a bit more about the other cases Dr. Burch had seen, and whether he had anything more to offer them in the way of options.

Will finally decided to speak. "Is it possible that Chet would recognize family at this point?"

The doctor turned to Amy and Andrea. They both answered there had been no reaction to their visits with Chet.

"It's variable, and I know how hard it is for people to say goodbye when there's no ability for a patient to respond. It's really a matter of doing what you believe Mr. Sutherland would want." He paused. "I understand, Mrs. Sutherland, you are the health care agent for your husband?"

Andrea could only nod. Her crying had overtaken her.

"I'm sorry. While he is unaware of his situation and unlikely to be in any pain, I don't believe he would be alive off of the ventilator, which, as an artificial means of keeping him alive, is a choice for you to discuss in the next day or so."

Amy spoke up. "I don't think any of us would like Dad to suffer with no hope in sight." She looked to both Will and Andrea.

Andrea spoke between sobs. "I don't want him to suffer needlessly, no."

Amy invited Will to weigh in. Will nodded, then asked Dr. Burch, "The decision, then, is whether or not to discontinue life support?"

"Yes."

Andrea blurted. "To *discontinue* it?" She collapsed into sobs. "Amy?"

Amy's voice trembled, but she said what needed to be said. "I'm sorry, Andrea, that's what a decision would be, if we made it . . . if you made it. Yes."

Will now knew exactly why Amy needed him on this call. "Dr. Burch, you've been very helpful. I think we'll need to have some more discussion among ourselves before we can make such a big decision. Thank you. We'll be in touch."

"I'm sorry. Just let me know if you need any further information. Goodbye."

Dr. Burch left the call, and nobody spoke. Will realized the three of them could be siblings, with their age range around ten years. Amy, the elder bossy sister, Andrea, the sheltered baby sister, and Will the middle child and peacemaker. The sisters were still tearful.

"Andrea, Amy, I'm so sorry it has come to this. What can I do to help here?"

"I can't do this. Chet makes the decisions, I don't. I can't even talk to him about what he wants," Andrea said.

"Have you ever talked about it? Any discussion about end of life or any written instructions?" Amy asked.

"No. Not really. I know they made him file something at his doctor's, putting me as the agent for his health in an emergency situation, but that was like a bureaucratic thing to do, no discussion about it. I had to do it for my last physical, as well." Andrea was now at least thinking about it.

Two unconnected facts collided in Will's mind. He remembered Amy had said Chet was putting his affairs in order. The other was that there was an email from Chet's attorney alluding to documents that had just been revised regarding his estate. Didn't estate documents include end-of-life wishes, healthcare wishes, etc.? He decided to take a sideways route. "Do you think Chet had anything in his legal papers? Papers that his attorney may have, that would shed light on his wishes?"

Amy jumped on it. "That's right. Usually, an attorney makes you get your end-of-life papers in order. Andrea, what do you think? Is that a possibility?"

"Maybe. I know Chet was doing some legal stuff to get ready for his retirement. But I'm not sure of any details." She sounded as if she was drowning again.

"Andrea, I think you may get some clarity on this if you reach out to the attorney Chet was working with. I assume he's someone you know?" He waited until Andrea nodded. "I'm not family, but I believe both of you should have another visit with your husband and father, to have another look at him before any big decision can be made. Am I right?"

Both women looked at him as if he had sent them life preservers. If there was anything Will knew how to do well, it was close a meeting with a clear action plan. They agreed to talk again late the next day.

He got up to stretch his legs and revisit the meeting. Had he succeeded in being helpful but not overstep his role as family friend and former trusted friend of the man in question? *Dear Lord, I hope so.*

CHAPTER 18

The first one awake, Will walked through the sleeping house with mortality on his mind. He thought hard about his moral compass. He had always thought he had one. After watching both parents succumb to cancer in his high school years, he knew he wanted to use the insurance money to educate himself and follow his interest into scientific research to help people. And he did.

Once the first success with a break-through medicine came about, he was interested in doing even more. With Charlotte's encouragement, he moved on and up to use his natural leadership skills and scientific know-how to launch more and more beneficial therapeutics. He felt driven to reach more people. And he did.

After he understood the machinations of the US pharmaceutical industry, he knew he needed to learn more about the industry beyond its borders. He took positions that would expose him to worldwide markets and how he could maximize the successes of medical breakthroughs and make them available to even more people. And he did.

Now, on the threshold of the top job at BioteKem, he was in a position to influence the future of one of the largest biomedical companies in the world. To help even more people.

He had enriched himself along the way. But his lifestyle wasn't over the top. Not like many who lived extravagant lives and paid more attention to stock prices than to their R&D investment. Chet Sutherland was the role model Will wanted to work with. He respected the man and grew to enjoy and thrive in their relationship. It was Chet who recruited Will into his role and his trust. Chet was a legend in the industry and the only man in it who Will wished to emulate. He wouldn't consciously do anything to damage that relationship. He remained puzzled about how things went awry, but any hope of a possible chance to clear the air with Chet seemed out of reach.

As Chet mentored Will and the knowledge transfer was complete, it was apparent Chet was lingering a bit, perhaps because he was worried about becoming irrelevant or because he would miss working with Will. They started to joke about it.

"Hell, Will, I could drop dead tomorrow and the company would be fine." Chet had his hand on Will's shoulder and said, "You're ready, son."

Will hated to face the truth. Before Chet had called him out for whatever he had done, he was impatient to be on top. Where was his moral compass now? And if Chet died, how could Will live without his forgiveness?

Once in the office, he was still pondering how he had so damaged Chet's faith in him when he heard a knock on his door. He looked up to see Pam Shields, fresh-faced and eager.

"Pam, good morning." He cleared his throat.

"Just wanted to follow up on the article. Did you have a chance to read it?"

"Yes." Will was glad to get this over with. "I don't see any need for BioteKem to make any comment. Better to let it run out on its own, okay?"

"Okay, but I think you should know there's been some follow-up on the story." She paused, a bit of melodrama in her manner. "Bella Davis has not been seen or heard from for over two weeks."

"What? How do you know all of this?"

"There was a follow-up note in BiotechNews this morning. I'll read it to you. 'Neither BioteKem nor Ms. Davis has come forward with a statement. Repeated attempts to reach Ms. Davis have failed. Her company states they haven't heard from her in over two weeks and are not aware of her whereabouts at this time.'"

Will got up and walked to the window and thought about when he had last seen Bella. The Sunday morning after the Friday night party when she had shown up unexpectedly at his office, which was just over two weeks ago.

"Dr. Franklin?" Pam finally asked.

"Yes, I heard you." He smiled in an attempt to cover his delay. "This news doesn't change my mind. No comment."

"Just wanted to be sure you knew this new bit. I'll keep you posted."

"You do that. Thanks." Will tried to keep his voice calm while his heart had moved to his throat and threatened his equilibrium. His business savvy told him this story would now evolve to one centering on Bella Davis and her disappearance. Selfishly, he hoped that would end any speculation about BioteKem in the rumored SEC investigation. However, he worried about what had happened to Bella. Why had she not been in touch with her office? Or had she been in touch, and they agreed on a narrative for the press? Why would they not want to dodge any other statement at this point? Had she been tipped off about the likely press attention and decided to hide out to avoid the pending SEC investigation noise, or was she holed up somewhere, alone?

He still thought of Bella with empathy. And more guilt. If

he had immediately turned that strange ambush in Philadelphia into what it should have been—an introduction to a possible mentee—perhaps he could have steered her in a direction that would have kept her out of trouble. If she was in trouble. He played out how the press would try to hunt her down.

Perhaps someone would theorize she was the victim of a cover-up or foul play to save her company from scrutiny. He blanched thinking someone would notify the police that she was missing, and he could be found to be one of the last people she had seen. He thought about the call from security the Sunday morning she had shown up at his building, and how he had allowed them to send her up. Surely, her name would be registered on the visitor roster. If he had resisted the ego boost of succumbing to this young woman's charms and channeled her attentions to her stated request of a mentor rather than a hookup, he wouldn't feel this guilt.

Now it appeared she needed guidance. *Or did she?* He broke out in a cold sweat when he considered the possibility she would try to get in touch with him.

He hit upon a new theory. Could she have set him up with Chet? Had she whispered in Chet's ear that Will was trading a favored position for her company with BioteKem in turn for her sexual favors? Did this fit? He hated to think he could have been victimized. He hated even more that Chet would buy it. How would Chet have been so incensed about Will's betrayal if it hadn't been so scandalous, so personal? Would an SEC investigator have evoked such an intense response from Chet?

The frisson of danger and attraction Bella had invoked in him from the start was still evident when she had appeared that morning. Yet every morning since, shame and regret of how he had been involved with her followed him. And now, worry for her as well as for himself. How would he explain her visit if it came to that?

He was glad Pam Shields agreed with his position. He didn't think BioteKem should be linked to the article in any way. Silence here was the right call. He would dodge any interviews about this. His throat seized considering how he could answer the question, "Do you know Ms. Davis?"

CHAPTER 19

Will finally admitted to himself it was time to seek help. As longtime general counsel for BioteKem, Larry Weisman was so well-connected in the industry that he could uncover and differentiate rumor, fact, and fiction in a way most could not, or find it among his wide network of contacts. Will remembered the advice Chet had given him about Larry.

"You can always count on his absolute discretion and loyalty." Will also knew he was adept at reading people and could sleuth out anxiety like a bloodhound after a fugitive.

When he sauntered into Will's office, Will brought him up to date on Chet's worsening condition.

"This is close to home," Larry reflected. "Chet is just five years older than I am. Hard to think we'd lose him so quickly to this terrible stroke." He gazed out the window, seeming to process this reality. "It's a personal loss for both of us. And for the company."

They chatted about the state of the world, the US government's response to the cyberattack, and the complexity of getting anything done across international borders to reduce the continuing supply chain disruption. Normally, Larry was fun to talk to, and Will had spent many an enjoyable business lunch with him and Chet over the past two years. But the mood was sedate, and they finally wound down to the assignment. Will was grateful Larry had not spoken aloud about what both were likely thinking—transition planning discussions would likely come soon.

"So, is there anything to that story about the SEC investigation?"

"Yes and no. But first let me tell you that my usual sources are hard to find right now. Things have really tightened up; not much buzz around about anything. Hack effect, I think. It took some time, but I did track down a hint of a live SEC investigation going on." Larry inhaled deeply before he started his lecture.

"As you know, SEC investigations can go on forever. They are conducted privately. Facts are developed to the fullest extent possible through informal inquiry, interviewing witnesses, examining brokerage records, reviewing trading data, and other methods. If there's a formal order of investigation, the division's staff may subpoena witnesses to testify and produce books, records, and other relevant documents. Following an investigation, SEC staff present their findings to the commission for its review. The commission can authorize the staff to file a case in federal court or bring an administrative action. In many cases, the commission and the party charged decide to settle a matter without trial."

"Yes, I have a broad understanding of their process. You said you think something is going on?" Will asked.

"I believe so. But it was more of a slip of the tongue than an affirmative yes," Larry cautioned.

"From a trusted source?" Will knew Larry well enough to know he wouldn't reveal more than he needed to.

"A new source."

"How can we confirm?"

"That will take more time. Could take lots more time."

Will weighed his options, then said, "Well, I think you should stay on it, then. What about the company. Were you able to find any connection between it and BioteKem?"

"Ah, that's the solid no. Nothing on paper between the two companies, and I did a pretty good search of the usual suspects within BioteKem to see if anyone knew of any interest in the start-up."

"Maybe look at the company a bit? See what's what with it?"

"Yeah, I haven't done that yet. Can do. This Bella Davis looks like she may have been a flight risk—"

"Yeah, what do you make of that?"

"Getting out while the getting's good is my bet."

Will tugged at his ear. "Larry, what do you think gave rise to this article?"

"So many beginner entrepreneurs and over-eager investors out there willing to shake the trees because they're desperate for some attention on their new company. This isn't the best attention, but it is something. I don't need to tell you how many of these newcos go belly up in their first years trying to get their name out there."

"Okay, stay in touch, my friend. I'll keep you in the loop about Chet."

Something almost magnetic in its power drew Will to Mass General. He told himself he was going there to find Clark, to thank him for his help, but as he drew near, he knew he wanted one last look at Chet. His dream was still alive in his mind.

Even as he asked himself what he would gain, his feet kept moving him forward. He got as far as the intensive care unit before he lost his nerve. But as he was turning to leave, Amy found him.

"It's over."

It took him a moment to recognize her. Dressed in sleek trousers and sweater with a colorful scarf, she looked different from the video call, more put together, as if she was prepared to make a strong case in defense of the action to be taken.

"I'm sorry. How did it go?" He reached out and took her trembling hands in his.

"Fast once we made the decision. Andrea and I each spent some time with him this morning, but I came back about an hour ago. We agreed he hadn't made any progress. Andrea faltered, but it helped that the attorney had called her with more specifics on Chet's wishes, which she then felt honor-bound to follow." She tilted her head up to keep the tears from spilling down her cheeks. "Thanks for thinking of that and bringing the attorney in, by the way; it made all the difference in how smoothly this went."

"I'm glad that helped the situation. How're Andrea and Danny doing?"

"Hard to say. God. It all feels so awkward. It makes me so damn mad." Her venting seemed therapeutic. "I feel like I lost my father just when we had finally reconciled and might have gained a new family only to have this strain of sudden death added to how we can relate!"

"I agree. It's a particularly cruel twist here for you. I'm sorry you're going through this." Will collected his thoughts before continuing. "For what it's worth, I admire how you've navigated the situation. Chet would be so grateful that you were involved in the way you were. Andrea and Danny are both lucky that you pushed ahead and helped them."

She laughed softly. "I have been described as pushy, but usually for the right reasons." She looked around and tucked a loose curl back into place. Listen, do you have time for a drink? I need to get out of here."

"Sure, let's go. There's a little spot just across the way. We can walk if that's okay?"

"Please, I need some air." Amy followed Will out the main hospital door, and they walked a block to a small pub.

After Amy ordered an old-fashioned and Will, still a bit shaky, decided on a club soda, he said, "I really believe you and your father's family will build a relationship from here. Sometimes, the stress of circumstances has that effect." Once he said those words, he felt the truth of them in his own life.

"I hope you're right. I'd like that. I don't want to screw this up." She took a breath and blew it out slowly, a lone tear tracking down one cheek. "I'm so happy Dad and I made things right between us before he passed. That was a blessing."

"Absolutely." *I'll never be able to make things right with Chet.*

"Did Dad ever tell you about why we were estranged for so long?" She seemed to want to talk, and Will leaned in.

"No, he didn't. He did share that his marriage to your mom was an unhappy one, and that her sudden death played a role, but no details."

"Yes. My dad suffered greatly through their marriage." She sipped her old-fashioned and swirled the glass to clink the ice. He didn't interrupt her soliloquy. "I was all of fifteen when she died, Danny's age, and I have a fifteen-year-old girl, Molly, so I see how impressionable that age is now.

"He fell in love with a vibrant woman who took him on a hell ride. She wasn't diagnosed with bipolar disorder until very late, and in the early years, Dad just enjoyed the mild manic periods and became scarce during the down times." She smiled at him. "You know better than most how busy he must have been during the rise of the industry. Travel, long days, and business dinners—he more or less disappeared to me as a parent for much of my childhood, at least as someone to rely on.

"My mom was a mess much of the time, but she was my mom. I now know there was an earlier suicide attempt when I was about ten that led to a hospitalization and diagnosis. After that, it was a matter of keeping her on her meds, which she didn't like, because they dulled the fun times and caused her to gain weight. She was vain in her appearance and a terrible flirt." Amy smiled.

"I think my dad's worst time of it was after she was diagnosed and there was a rift between them about control of her mind. She felt he didn't love her in all of her many facets. He felt she was dangerous to herself and possibly others when she was off her meds. Of course, I was aware of the tug-of-war."

Amy hesitated and exhaled loudly. "Anyway, that went on for years. I developed an eating disorder—the classic attempt to keep control of your body when your world is out of control." Again, she clinked the ice, and took a deep breath. "I didn't learn this until later, but she was pregnant with another man's child when she took her life and the baby's." Her voice broke.

"Dad knew she was sleeping around and couldn't really stop her. She had her own separate life really, as did he. When she told him she was pregnant, expecting him to be pleased and to pass it off as his, he told her the baby couldn't be his because he had a vasectomy after her diagnosis. He had kept the information from her." She watched his reaction as Will gaped at her. "I know—totally messed up."

Will asked the bartender for another old-fashioned for Amy, and in that instant knew he would be driving her home in her car; he would sit and listen to her for as long as she needed to vent.

Amy straightened in the booth, as if to strengthen her backbone. "So, there was not a healthy dynamic to fall back on after her suicide, and Dad dumped all of it on my adolescent shoulders. In today's vernacular, we would call it 'oversharing.' It was too much for me. I had a breakdown of sorts and retreated into myself. When I went off to college, I left my dad. Of course, he was not in good shape himself. He told me it took him years to get right again. Later, he tried to reach out to me, but I couldn't handle it."

She sobbed lightly. "I regret that now. I wish we had been able to lean on each other earlier. I'm a psychiatric nurse. It took me years of therapy to understand my own psyche, and years of training and experience to forgive my mother her excesses. But it took me the longest time to forgive my father for not keeping some of the sad tale from me. Do you know what finally did it?"

"What?"

"When Danny turned fifteen, Dad realized how unfair it had been to unload all of the emotional garbage on me, treating me as an adult, not a kid. He apologized. He finally got it."

"This is a heartbreaking story."

"Yes, it is. Think of all of the lost years. The pain for him, for me. The joy lost. So, you see, I'm grateful that Dad and I reconciled before he passed, but very sad it was so late in coming."

"I'm so sorry."

"Thank you." She blew out stifled air, lifted her head high, and pulled her shoulders back again. "The truth is, I still grieve for my mother. But I grieve even more for my unborn sibling. That was a secret I could not bear." A sob escaped her, and her voice was now just a whisper. "My father finally came to realize that dumping all of that on me when I was fifteen and too young to handle it was a mistake. A tough life lesson that almost destroyed our relationship."

They both grew quiet, and Will handed her his handkerchief as her tissues were totally limp.

Finally, Amy said, "Thank God my dad forced the issue and got through my defenses before it was too late."

Amy seemed calmer but drained after telling her story to Will and happily agreed to his offer to drive her home.

He had missed a text message while driving Amy home and read it in his Uber ride home.

Robin Warren here. Call me in the morning.
News about Davis.

He realized how exhausted he was when this message didn't even break through it. He used his last bit of energy to climb up to bed in a quiet house, home after a trying day.

Sleep came fast, but relief was still out of reach.

CHAPTER 20

Before Will parted for home the previous night, Amy had floated the idea of getting the three families together the next day for a comfort food dinner to surround Andrea and Danny with love and support before they had to face the entire world. While Will was open to it, he didn't think Amy was in any shape to make plans, so he dismissed it until he walked into the kitchen the next morning, a Saturday, and found Charlotte on the phone with her. When he walked in, she registered him in her peripheral vision and pointed to the phone, mouthing *Amy*.

"It sounds like a nice idea. I'm sure they're reeling." Charlotte hesitated, then added, "Have you checked in with Andrea? Maybe it's too much for her?" Charlotte listened and seemed to agree with whatever Amy said, then started to open cupboards.

"Yes, okay then, we'd be happy to be there in support. How about if I make mac and cheese—the Martha Stewart recipe that is appealing to adults as well as kids? Mine love it." Charlotte chuckled as she listened. "Wow—three fifteen-year-olds in the same house—that should be fun."

Recalling how emotionally raw Amy had been last night, Will smiled to himself at the realization that the opportunity to vent might have helped her face what was coming.

"Of course not, we don't want Andrea to worry about any of it. 4:00 p.m., then? Great, see you there." Charlotte ended the call and turned to Will. "Wow, she's a take-charge woman—I like her already. She thinks it'll be good to get the three families together. I get the impression she wants some help to ease in with Andrea and Danny." She grabbed a mug from the cupboard. "Ready for coffee?"

Will had given her minimal information last night before he crashed, and while the news had not been unexpected, Charlotte's response had surprised him.

"It seems the only way it could have ended. I'm glad the suffering is over."

Will knew her empathy was directed to the family, but for one selfish moment, amid his cloud of self-loathing and doubt, he wished she could have included him in her caring.

Now, in the bright morning light, over coffee, he relayed to Charlotte the sad tale of Amy and Chet's estrangement. This time, her response did not surprise him at all.

"I like the woman even more. What strength of character she has. She'll be good for Andrea." Charlotte pulled out a block of cheddar cheese from the refrigerator. "Wow, that's a new dimension of Chet; we keep learning about him, don't we?"

It was a throw-away comment from Charlotte but struck him. *Did I ever really know Chet?* He puzzled over Amy's perspective. She thought her dad should have kept the secret and protected her. But which one? The suicide, the pregnancy, her mother's diagnosis? How would that have worked?

Here again, he was unable to talk to Chet, unable to decipher his motivations or even validate Amy's experience. It wasn't any of his business. The more he thought about it, the more he realized how complex a man Chet was. Viewed as a good and honorable man by most, and finally forgiven by his daughter, Chet had no doubt lived with his own demons for a long time.

He was struck by how angry Chet had been at him when last they met. Too angry to explain what transgressions he had committed to warrant being fired. Too angry to discuss why. Chet was not perfect; he knew that now. Nobody was. He remembered his words.

"I expected more from you."

And I expected more from you. The thought floated into his head and stayed. Will had been feeling nothing but guilt based on Chet's accusations, since they had been hurled at him. Now, he carried the burden Chet had left him, unbidden. No recourse to settle it. The thrum of anxiety that had taken up residence in his body since that short meeting was still with him, causing increasing self-doubt. Will had started to believe he had done terrible things, even if he didn't know exactly what those were. *Except for Bella.* Was she the missing piece in Chet's rant? He needed to unwind the noose Chet had been ready to hang him with.

Once Charlotte had finalized their evening plans, Will excused himself to return Robin Warren's call. He was curious about what she would say. Worry followed him into his office. *What if my name is in print as a target of the SEC investigation?*

First, he checked the online news outlet for anything new. There were several new posts, but repetitive with what had already been posted. A couple of hateful posts about Bella herself, calling her a princess who might be losing her kingdom. Weird misogyny, Will thought. Nothing from Robin Warren with an update, and no post from the company itself about the whereabouts of Bella Davis. If this was a serious investigation, he assumed the company would have a public relations firm dealing with damage control and handling all communication.

He also checked a few search engines with Met-Med and SEC but came up with nothing. So far, this story, based on a rumor, seemed confined to this one online news outlet and the one reporter. He took some comfort in that, although the underlying anxiety never left him.

Robin Warren picked up. "Mr. Franklin. If you're still interested in the BioTechNews article, I found something interesting."

"Is there something new?" He tried to sound matter-of-fact and hide any desperation.

"No, not really. Just something rather interesting."

"Go on."

"Well, remember I told you that my source was anonymous?"

"Yes."

"I tried to reach her again after you and I talked, but she evidently called from a burner phone. So that made me more curious. I did some research on Met-Med, which turns out to be a relatively low-rent operation. Their offices are located in a strip mall in New Jersey. Anyway, I turned my attention to Bella Davis." She waited for a response.

"And?"

"And she's all over social media. YouTube videos and a few fancy speeches to industry groups here and there." Robin's excitement came through the line, her words coming faster as he imagined her watching video as she spoke. "She's really magnetic on video. Her charisma seems to jump right out and capture an audience." She waited for a response from Will that didn't come. She continued. "Anyway, here's the thing—Bella Davis's voice is the voice of my source."

Will's facial muscles went slack and his mouth fell open. Bella Davis had never ceased to surprise him. *Why would she do that? What next?* He measured his tone. "Are you sure? And if that's true, what do you think that means, Ms. Warren?"

"Well, I'm not a forensic investigator, but it sure sounds like the same person. When she called me, she used almost a stage whisper, and that, of course, is not how she sounds when she gives a speech to a group, but in some of her shorter sound bites, I detected the familiar tone." Robin was exhilarated, proud of her finding. "I don't have a clue what it means, but it must mean something, right?"

Will forced a light laugh. "I really have no idea. Has she shown up anywhere yet?"

"No, and her company is not taking calls."

"That says something right there, doesn't it? Anyway, thanks for the update, Ms. Warren. I have a call coming in that I need to take."

He remembered how he had been worried about her just the other day. In an instant, any empathy he had felt for Bella Davis went cold. He was determined to focus on solving this mystery before it drove him crazy. He couldn't properly grieve for his mentor and friend without understanding what had led to such a turn of trust on Chet's part. Right now, his mind was preoccupied with concern for Chet's family. He made a mental list of things to discuss with Andrea, at the right time. Not tonight; tonight was about family.

───────◇◇◇───────

On the drive to the Sutherlands, Tish asked, "Dad, what do we say to Danny tonight? What's it like to lose a parent when you're still a kid?"

"Well, it's hard. I lost both of my parents within three years. My mom to breast cancer and my dad to blood cancer. They suffered a lot before they died, and it was excruciating to watch."

"That must have been horrible. How did you do it?" Tish asked.

"It was very hard, and it still hurts. I think that's why I went into biomedical research. To try to solve medical problems so people didn't have to suffer. I feel good about that. I also learned I can handle hard things. We all can when we need to. And Danny will, too."

Charlotte added, "Just be his friend. He may not want to talk much about it tonight, so take the lead from him."

When they arrived, Charlotte led the family into the Sutherlands' house. Will and the kids carried the food. "Andrea, we're here!"

Andrea hugged Charlotte, and Danny greeted them shyly as Amy and her daughter emerged from the kitchen.

Amy introduced herself and Molly, explaining her son, Jay, was away at college.

Tish, never shy, said, "I'm confused. So how are you all related again?"

Danny responded, "Well, Amy is my half-sister, and Molly is my . . . is her daughter." He sounded a little flummoxed, and then started to chuckle, with the others joining in.

It didn't take long before they were all speaking at once, over one another, until Andrea finally said, "Thank you all for coming. Danny and I are so grateful that Amy planned this evening for us all to get together. We needed to be around people who cared for Chet and care for us now that he is gone." She started to tear up and took Danny's hand. "Let's eat, shall we?"

Later, Andrea led them into the living room. The kids had vanished to the family room to play video games. "Let's get comfortable, and bring the wine?" She curled up on the couch. Amy joined her there and said, "Is it terrible to feel relieved that it's over?"

Andrea looked at Amy and exhaled. "God, I hope not, because I do."

With the floodgates now open, Charlotte and Will listened as both widow and daughter described the last days of anguish, the ups and downs of Chet's condition as he seemed to wither in front of them. By the end of their narrative, they were finishing each other's sentences. At one point, Amy handed Andrea a tissue and she held Amy's hand.

"Amy, thank you for all of your help. I know I wouldn't have been able to do it without you. I apologize for not letting you in earlier . . . I just didn't . . ."

"No apology needed. I'm just glad we connected while it still mattered." Amy's voice wobbled. "And thanks, Will, for facilitating that for us."

Andrea added, "If it hadn't been for Will at the beginning . . ." Her eyes went to the ceiling. "All I can say is there was good reason for Chet to trust you." Her eyes bored into Will's. "I can never thank you enough for being there every step of the way. You're the best."

Will swallowed hard, trying to curb his own feelings of confusion. "I'm glad I could help."

Andrea gazed at Charlotte. "My friend Charlotte, your help in keeping us fed here and listening to my meanderings when you visited, well, what can I say. You personified what a friend is, and I am forever grateful to you as well."

Charlotte said, "You and Amy have been through hell these past weeks, and I'm so happy that we were able to help you both." She gestured to open her arms to both women on the couch. "It is great to see the two of you together, and isn't it amazing that you have each other now?"

As they continued with lighter chatter, Andy came in to ask if he could have another brownie. When Charlotte joined Amy in the kitchen, Andrea asked Will to stay with her for a minute.

Once they were alone, she confided, "That was the hardest thing I've ever done, Will. I can't believe he's gone. I know this is hard for you, too, but I expect we have some decisions to make in the next day or two?"

"Yes." Will knew certain things couldn't wait. "But first, you need to take care of yourself and Danny. Any plans for a service can be left for a few days. Maybe a communication out about Chet's death would make sense. Would you like me to have the BioteKem communications office come up with something for your review? If we don't get something out, there will be more guesswork than fact out there."

"That's a good idea. Could we also have Amy review it?"

"Of course. That makes sense."

"I'm so glad Chet was able to move beyond his guilt for whatever happened between him and his daughter and reach out for reconciliation. I know it bothered him, although he wasn't ever able to tell me about it. It comforts me that he didn't die with unfinished business there. Amy and I had a good cry over that."

"I'm glad it worked out, and I'm sure Chet would be pleased it's happening," Will said. "Since you've had a conversation with your family attorney about his final wishes, I assume he will be ready to help you with any planning as needed, when you're ready."

"Yes, he's already made a call to me. He said no hurry, which is good."

"You're raising a great kid in Danny. He's doing okay?"

"Yes, I think he's relieved I have Amy around as support." Andrea smiled. "Thanks for helping us get through this far." Andrea rose, and they rejoined the group in the family room, the evening naturally coming to an end.

Jackets and cookware were retrieved, and the three families gathered to say their goodbyes. Amy's eyes glistened as she thanked everyone individually with a warm hug. Will appraised the relaxed group of kids and adults and realized there could be a growing bond among the families.

Can something good arise from this strange chapter with Chet?

CHAPTER 21

The following Monday, Will asked Pam Shields to work up a draft press release for Andrea and Amy to review and called a short exec team meeting to announce the death. Very few of them had a current working relationship with Chet, as he had been more figurehead than active in the company for the past few years.

Larry Weisman knew him best and shared a story or two. Then he summed it up with, "They don't come any finer. An honorable gentleman in his personal and professional lives."

With Amy's story about her mom still fresh in his mind, Will thought about the generous assessment, but he shook off his rush to judgment. *Stop! You don't know anything for a fact, and neither did Chet know anything about you for a fact. And just because someone makes a blunder, it doesn't make them dishonorable.*

He spent the remainder of the day calling board members and other VIPs who needed to hear from him personally about Chet's death. Since Will was long recognized as in charge in Chet's absence, there wasn't an action needed to affirm leadership in the short term. Consideration of executing the succession plan could wait for a bit.

He made twelve calls to board members and got through to most of them. Will fielded lots of questions about Chet's stroke and treatment. He did his best to respect Chet's privacy, but he was in an odd position. He was aware of all of it, had arranged for the hospital, the support of his family, the reunion of his estranged daughter with his wife, even helping them navigate a plan for end of life. He kept with a general script of less is more. Chet's family situation was private, and the illness was tragic at any age, especially with Chet's looming retirement to be enjoyed.

He did this for a man who wanted him fired. He remained mystified about why a fling with Bella could be the only reason. *It can't be, but then why?*

Will reviewed the facts. Chet's plan to pull the board together to take emergency action to fire him had not happened. None of the board members knew Chet was intent on firing him. Was he safe? Could he relax now?

No, he couldn't. He checked Chet's devices for any additional posts to the online article in BioTechNews. He found a new post.

Bella Davis was sighted boarding a charter flight to the Virgin Islands almost three weeks ago in the company of Rocco Barletti, an Italian biotech investor.

He was puzzling over this news when Miles Fortney called. Miles was a former BioteKem board member who knew Chet well and had been on the board when Will was recruited in.

"I can't believe he's gone, Will. This is such a crazy time. The man was starting to enjoy a well-deserved pre-retirement lap, and poof . . . ended by a crazy stroke. I'm sorry to ask because I'm sure you've been working the phones for the last couple of days, but could you walk me through how it went down?"

Miles was close to Chet and sounded so eager to empathize with his friend, even in death, that Will detailed the twenty plus days leading to Chet's death. Even now as he relayed the story, he felt tears forming and his fists tightening.

Miles had interrupted a few times to ask for more detail, but when Will had finished, he made a comment that caused Will to gasp. "You know I saw him just before he got sick. At the Royal Sonesta Hotel, in the dining room. Looked like a business lunch." He spoke gently, remembering his friend. "With a beautiful young woman. I remember that." Will knew Miles was smiling now. "They looked so intense; I decided not to interrupt. Now, of course, I wish I had." He cleared his throat. "It's funny what you remember about these things. I remember Chet looked dapper but not happy. The woman looked . . . assertive maybe, and she had this bright red lipstick."

Will couldn't speak but listened closely.

"Anyway, I wish now that I had approached and chatted with Chet. It would have been the last time."

Will was careful to modulate his voice. "You had no idea who the woman was?"

"None, just that she was a looker. They didn't seem to be having much fun." Miles was wistful. "I want to remember Chet golfing or goofing off and having fun!"

"Yes, of course, you should do that." Will ended the conversation before he blurted out any more questions about the lunch date. *I know enough.*

In the past forty-eight hours, Will had learned Bella may have been Robin Warren's anonymous source, Bella had boarded a flight to the Virgin Islands with an Italian investor, and now, if Miles' description could be believed, Bella might have had a contentious lunch with Chet in the days leading up to the conference. Just before Chet lost his trust in Will.

How much of this was connected or coincidental? Will prided himself on having a cool head in business. Not to rush to judgment, to gather facts, use data, take control of the information gathered, and then make a decision. However, he was having a hard time staying cool on this most personal assault.

What decision could he reach putting together the facts that he knew? Bella must be the missing link, but how would he gather more facts about her? Should he hire an investigator to find her and uncover what dealings she may have had with Chet? He knew better than to call her. He was already caught in her web and trying to get out. What could he do?

His list for tomorrow: Bella, Bella, Bella.

CHAPTER 22

In his office, Will took a few minutes between meetings to call Charlotte, who should have been home after taking Tish back to Deerfield Academy after spring break. He recalled the emotional send-off that morning. Danny's loss of his father had hit her hard, and she had given him a tighter hug than usual.

"Hello." Charlotte's voice came through from her car connection.

"Charlotte, you're still on the road? I was just calling to find out how drop-off went. All good?"

"Yes. I just got delayed coming back. I'm glad you called. You'll need to pick Andy up from Trevor's house tonight on your way home."

"Of course."

"Trevor's mom knows he may stay for dinner. I wasn't sure when you could pick him up."

"I'll leave early and be there by five. How's that?"

"Fine. Andy will like that. I'll see you at home. And Will?"

"Yes?'

"We need to talk." Charlotte hung up.

Will, constantly looking for signs that his relationship with Charlotte was salvageable, hung his head. Worry consumed him as he scrolled through his contacts looking for Trevor's address. He did not want to have to call his wife back when she had just asked him for an everyday parent task that he rarely performed and should be competent to handle.

Merilee knocked her signature code, two short and one long, on his office door before entering.

"Hi boss, got a minute?"

"Always. What's up?"

"You know how we've been handling Mr. Sutherland's mail?" She waited for his nod to continue. "I've been sorting through it and pulling out what I thought you should see. Opening most of it. We didn't think it should be delivered to his house, given he wasn't there, but now?"

"Good question. It was the right call not to bombard Andrea with all of it. Is there anything that looks time sensitive?" He saw her shuffling through papers and waited.

"Nah, mostly industry newsletters, you know, the usual stuff. Hold on a sec . . ." She perused one piece of mail closely. "Ah, there's an official-looking letter with an SEC stamp on it. Could be just filler, though."

Will's heart fluttered. Could he grab it out of her hands without looking like a crazy man? He bought time with a question. "What's the postmark date?"

"Not readable, looks like this was smushed with something that got wet. Sorry."

"Okay, then, open it." Will forced himself to breathe while she used the letter opener to tear the paper.

"Got it. The date is about two weeks ago. Mr. Sutherland was still alive. It's confirmation of an interview scheduled for next week. No subject noted for the interview. The usual mystery around the SEC, I guess."

Will's shoulders dropped. "Interesting."

"Would you like me to call to notify them of Mr. Sutherland's passing? There's a number listed."

"Ah, maybe I should do it. It may be something I can handle on the phone with them quickly."

"Of course." Merilee handed him the letter, and Will reached out to take it, half-expecting it to burn his hands.

"Is there other mail to Chet, anything that looks personal?"

"Not really." She made fast work of the remaining letters.

"And going forward?"

"Now that news of Chet's death is out, that should stop anything that may be active for BioteKem's purposes." He didn't think Bella would send anything by snail mail if she hadn't tried to communicate with him digitally. "Let's just continue to monitor it for a couple more weeks before we decide." *How long will my world be topsy-turvy?*

As always, Merilee's equanimity calmed him, and he kept her in the office for a while just catching up. He needed a breather before processing this next puzzle piece.

Will was preparing for his 3:30 p.m. meeting when Larry Weisman peeked in. He hoped he was there with news of Met-Med and not to start the inevitable succession conversation they would need to have very soon. "Hey Larry, what's up?"

Larry was unusually soft-spoken. "How are you doing today? I've been remiss not to acknowledge your own loss. I know how close you were to Chet and now, carrying this crazy cyberattack burden and leading the company through it, and helping his wife deal with everything . . . it's got to be heavy for you."

"Thanks, Larry, I appreciate that. It's hard to believe we've lost him."

"Well, if you need to take some time off, I know people would understand."

As general counsel, Larry served both the board and its chief executive. Will interpreted the gesture as evidence Larry had already been in contact with the board on succession timing, and this was them offering their support. "Thank you, but I'm okay. I'm sure the board is interested in moving forward soon on leadership, but I think it would be best for all of us if we allow Andrea a little time to consider a plan to honor Chet's passing before any announcement is made." *And I'd like to close out the mystery first.*

"Agreed. We do think that's best. Unless the market gets jumpy, that is."

"Of course." Will had been watching the stock carefully and didn't see an issue. "Andrea is still processing the past few weeks. I'm also in touch with Chet's daughter. I'll be talking with them tomorrow to see where they are on everything."

"Sounds good." Larry moved on, his speech pattern now at a faster clip. "So, I have some new info on the other thing. Do you have time to go through it now?"

"Yes. What have you found out about the company?"

"Nothing from them. They're locked up and shut down. Nobody answering any phones. The attorney of record listed is evidently off the job as of three months ago."

"So, they really weren't selling product at all?"

"Not that I know of. Proof of concept is all I hear. Lots of talk about not much is the way I would sum it up. Seems our girl Bella was the star of the show, and she's a no-show now."

"What do you mean?"

"I don't know if you've been following that online news outlet that posted the article originally, but I check it now and then. A couple of days ago, there was a post about Bella Davis." Larry pulled a piece of paper from his file folder. "It says she was 'sighted boarding a charter flight to the Virgin Islands almost three weeks ago, in the company of Rocco Barletti, an Italian biotech investor.'"

With a hint of feigned surprise, Will raised an eyebrow. "Interesting development?" *He's catching up to what I read already. Good, I want him leading on this, not me.*

"Yes, having them seen together adds to the evidence of a connection between them. I've had some luck finding information on Rocco Barletti. Seems he's a very rich guy who's been allowed to spend the family fortune however he wishes. I can't verify it, but I would guess that he has or was about to make a sizable contribution to Met-Med. His office in Milan says he's out of the country on business."

"Do we know what the connection is between the two of them?"

"If you're asking if they're romantic partners, I couldn't say for sure. I did find his name on the attendance list for the Annual Global Healthcare Summit, and Bella Davis's name was on the list as well. She's a beautiful young woman, and he's a rich middle-aged man." Larry raised an eyebrow. "Wouldn't surprise me. It's a pairing as old as time itself."

"Are you able to trace any money from him to Met-Med?"

"No. Met-Med is a private holding. I'd like to shake that loose through an investor, but I haven't found any names yet, other than this guy. Right now, we're checking to see where he's staying."

"You're sure he's still in the Virgin Islands?"

"No, but if we find him, we'll try to talk to him. And her if we can find her."

Will considered the risks ahead. "Barletti maybe, but why would Bella Davis ever agree to talk to you?"

"Right now, it's hard to know what her interests would be." Will knew Larry never liked to admit defeat. "You still want me to dig, or should we let it go? I've not seen any more press interest. Maybe it's passed by us?"

"I may have agreed to let it go yesterday, but just now Merilee unearthed a letter to Chet from the SEC to confirm an interview with him for next week."

"That's a surprise. Chet didn't mention anything to me." Larry sat up straighter in his chair. "Typical SEC to drop out of the sky with something like that. I take it there was no subject referenced in the letter?"

"There wasn't. If it's anything to do with this Met-Med, I think we better continue to investigate a bit."

"I agree." Larry was quick with his response. "Let me handle the SEC letter. I can call and do some fishing, see what's what?"

"What do you think is the better strategy, for you to call officially as general counsel or for me to bumble into it as Chet's friend and colleague picking up any pieces due to his untimely passing?"

"Under no circumstances would I advise you to make the call. If you're thinking to keep it under the radar, it should be Merilee, but that will just eat up time and not get us any information. I should be the one to take it up the ladder there to find out what's going on. Chet would have come to me as soon as he got his letter, so that's what we should do."

"Thanks Larry." Will blew out the breath he was holding and stood up. *Thank God Larry is paid handsomely to keep them out of trouble.* "Stay in touch."

CHAPTER 23

Will and Andy were finishing dessert when Charlotte arrived home. After she hugged her son, she said to Will, "Thanks for the last-minute help. Pancakes for dinner?"

"And frozen vegetables!" Andy said.

Charlotte laughed. "Sounds good!" She left the kitchen with her briefcase and headed to her office, near the nanny suite. "Carry on."

After Andy had gone to bed, Charlotte asked Will to join her in the family room. She brought a bottle of wine and a couple of glasses. Mindful of the last sit-down they had had alone in this room, Will forced a different seating configuration than before and turned on a second lamp in an attempt to dull the memory of that night. His wife's face in profile, in the dark, still haunted him.

He sat stone-faced, expecting the worst. Charlotte poured him a glass of wine. "You look frozen in place. Are you okay?"

"I am. Are you?" He tried to swallow his doubt. "Are we?"

"Yes, I'm fine." She paused, then added slowly. "I just thought we should have a check-in. I'm not ready to discuss the status of 'us' being okay. It's way too early to think about that yet." Charlotte sat on the far side of the couch, facing him. "These past few days have been busy because of the lead-up to Chet's death. Plus, I've been trying to get my arms around a complicated new case."

Will's pulse quickened at the news of a new case. That explained her business manner on the phone with him and the delay getting home. When Charlotte had a new client looking for a clinical trial that may help find a cure for their particular situation, she was all business and single-minded in her pursuit. She was great at it.

Will let out a huge breath. "Tell me about it."

"Well, it's new. But it came to me from a Tufts contact, a new source. A family from Rockport in Essex County. I stopped there to meet them on my way back from Deerfield. I'm just beginning to work on it."

"Good for you, Charlotte. I'm so proud of the work you do to help these families." Will smiled broadly. His eyes lifted to his wife's face. Her features now softened as she accepted the compliment. Did he see a glint of recon-ciliation there?

"Thank you." Charlotte changed the subject quickly, and curled her body into itself, away from him. "I wanted to find out what the latest is about the mystery, the SEC, etc. What's happening?"

Will sat up straighter. "Yes, there have been some devel-opments. Robin Warren called to tell me she believes Bella was her anonymous tipster leading to the online news article about the SEC. Then there was an additional post reporting Bella was sighted leaving the country with an Italian investor."

"This is like something out of the tabloids or a movie plot." Charlotte took a sip of wine.

Oh, good, he thought, *this means she hasn't been fol-lowing the story. If Charlotte thinks it's ludicrous that I am involved with any SEC irregularities, then she's in my corner.* He added, "Today I got a call from a former BioteKem board member who told me he had seen Chet having lunch with a young woman just before he was reported to be ill."

"And?"

"And his description of the young woman sounded like Bella Davis. Plus, he reported that it appeared to be an unpleasant meeting. I believe his word was 'intense.'"

Charlotte leaned back to reflect before she spoke again. "You have Chet's phone and computer. Did you ever find any trace of Bella Davis communicating with him on either device?"

"No." Will tried to track her thoughts. If they had met for lunch, wouldn't there have been a digital footprint of a confirmation or date on his calendar?

"That's odd." Charlotte knitted her eyebrows together. "But maybe . . . When Amy and I were doing kitchen cleanup after our dinner at Andrea's, we chatted about her last several months of slow reconciliation with her dad. She mentioned how he frequently texted her. That's how he set up meetings with her. Did you find any of those texts on his phone?"

"No, nothing." Will looked at his wife and they spoke as one.

"Chet had another phone."

CHAPTER 24

■■■■■■■■■■■■■■■■■■■■

Refracted light bounced toward Will and might have blinded him had he not looked down quickly. He chased away the memory of the last similar experience with Chet at the boathouse and followed his hostess. Andrea led him to the back of her house to a room filled to the corners with flowers and plants delivered in the last few days, the cloying smell so overpowering that Will sneezed.

"Please tell Charlotte again how much I appreciated her helping keep us in groceries these past few weeks. I called her myself this morning to tell her I was able to take back shopping duty. She was so sweet to do it." She handed Will a cup of coffee as they settled in her sunroom with Amy. "Look at this weather. It's so sunny and beautiful. I can't believe we're meeting to plan Chet's funeral on such a lovely day. I think it's a sign that Chet is sending us his love. He did often say 'life is for the living.'" She turned quickly to study the landscape out the window. "Perhaps I'll get there at some point."

Amy spoke like the psychiatric nurse she was. "Grieving is a long process. Especially given how sudden Dad's death was, it will take all of us some time."

"How about you, Amy, how are you doing?" Will wanted to give Andrea a minute to collect herself.

"My schedule is always fairly busy. But I've taken some time off for the first time in a long while." Amy smiled.

Andrea poured herself some more coffee from the pot on the table and then said, "You know, I have to admit it feels like I've gained a sister not a stepdaughter. That's the blessing of this whole situation." She said to Will, "Amy and I have started talking about the service, but we could use your input."

"Of course. I'm glad you brought it up. What are your thoughts so far?"

"Scattered, actually." She frowned slightly. "I've been in touch with our minister but haven't made any plans yet. I'm confused about whether we should have one large funeral or just a small ceremony for family."

"Let's think that through. I know there will be lots of people who will want to honor him in some way. Not just BioteKem people, but Chet is well-known and respected in the larger industry. He's been such a figure in building biotech. Have you thought about that?"

"Yes, I know we need to acknowledge his contribution to the industry and allow people to attend a service of remembrance. I like that idea. I wish I knew what he would want. It's not a topic of conversation that came up." The newly minted widow folded her hands as she reflected, "I know Chet always appreciated the ceremony and ritual of a funeral service. He believed it helped people with closure."

"Is it fair to ask BioteKem to help with planning that type of service?" Amy asked.

"Yes, of course. We can help and should." Will reassured them both. "Are you thinking of a separate family service in addition?"

Andrea addressed Amy. "Gosh, it would be really small, wouldn't it? Just you and your kids and me. My sister in California may come, but you have no other cousins or anybody, right?"

"Right." Amy reached out to pat Andrea's shoulder. "Andrea, this is your decision, but I don't see the need for a separate family funeral. I think we could plan a meaningful service to honor Dad's contributions as well as to help the family with closure."

"Yes, I think you're probably right about that." She sounded relieved. "I also have some thoughts about memorials. Chet always felt strongly about contributing to the scholarship fund that the two of you started at BioteKem for STEM kids. I'd like to designate that fund."

"I love that idea, and so would Chet," Will said.

"Andrea," Amy asked, "how about a memorial gift to your community theater in his name as well? I know you were both involved."

Andrea's eyes got big, and she gasped. "What a wonderful idea. How lovely for you to suggest it. Thank you." She collapsed into sobs and excused herself, leaving Amy and Will alone in the sunroom.

"This funeral planning is tough on her," Will said. "You knew exactly how to personalize her own loss through that memorial gift idea. Well done, Amy."

"She deserves it. I'm not sure she would have thought of it on her own." Amy looked past Will to the sunroom door before adding, in a stage whisper, "I got a call from Dad's lawyer yesterday." She seemed hesitant. "He asked me if I'd be executor of Dad's estate."

"Good. That seems right."

"Well, he also told me that until the day before Dad was hospitalized, he had your name in mind. Do you know anything about that?"

"Really? I have no idea." Will shook his head as he took in the news. *How many more surprises can there be?* "Your dad never discussed any of it with me, never asked me to serve as executor of his estate. I can only guess at his reasoning; perhaps he contemplated that prior to you and he reconciling? But after that, it made sense to him to name you, a family member, as opposed to me?"

"I get that, but I can poke holes in that theory easily. Dad and I had reconciled, that's true. Dad talked to me about his estate, but he also told me he planned to name a trusted friend as executor. He didn't want Andrea to feel she was second fiddle to his daughter. Thought someone out of the family would be better. When I talked to the attorney, I guessed at who the trusted friend was, and the attorney reluctantly didn't deny it when I mentioned you."

"I wasn't aware of any of his thinking on this, so haven't a clue." Will's mind was spinning again. "Probably doesn't matter. I assume you're willing to serve as executor?"

"Of course, but it is curious, isn't it? Changing his mind like that, just the day before he got sick." Will heard Andrea coming. Amy finally spoke again. "Did you two have a falling out, like suddenly?"

Fortunately, before she pressed Will for an answer, Andrea rejoined them. *A falling out? How can I explain what I don't understand myself?*

Will worked hard to keep his head on topic when Andrea returned, and they finalized how they would proceed with the funeral planning. As she walked him through the house to show him all of the flowers in the living room, they passed Chet's office, the door ajar. Will glanced in and his eyes homed in on a framed picture of himself and Chet. Both men were smiling broadly. Chet's arm was around Will.

Will stopped so abruptly that Amy, following behind, practically ran over him. "Oh, gosh Amy, sorry." He turned quickly to steady her. "It's just that picture. Such a happy day that was. We were celebrating having raised over $1 million that year for the foundation." Will walked in to get a closer look, and enveloped in all things Chet, he started to cry softly. Andrea and Amy both hugged him, adding their own tears. When they finally disentangled, each of them was red-faced, and Andrea passed around a box of tissues.

Driving out of their neighborhood, Will knew that expressing his grief with Andrea and Amy would ease his anxiety only momentarily. While still in Chet's office, he had surreptitiously scanned the surfaces looking for another phone Chet may have used. He knew that if Andrea and Amy had both left him there for any time at all, he would have searched every drawer and crevice, still hunting for more clues.

CHAPTER 25

Sometime after midnight, Will woke up in a sweat, unable to breathe. He scrambled out of bed and to the deck of the bedroom, gasping for cold night air. After several minutes of desperate air hunger, he registered sleet on his face coming down as slivers of cold steel.

"What are you doing out there?" Charlotte's panicky voice broke through, but he was still fighting for breath. By the time she got to him, he was finally able to squeak out, "Can't breathe."

As sleet pelted both of them on the frigid April night, Charlotte worked to loosen his iron grip on the deck railing. Unresponsive to her efforts, Will's breathing started to regulate but his body began to collapse into loud convulsive sobs interrupted by jagged gulps for air. Finally, his body crumpled, and Charlotte was able to remove his hands, but he was now dead weight on the floor.

As best she could, she covered his body with hers, repeating the words of comfort she used with her children when they were hurt. "It's okay. It will be okay. You're okay," while she stroked his back, then his cheek as he finally focused on her face.

Finally, between sobs, he said, "No, it won't be. I've betrayed you and failed Chet. It won't ever be okay again."

"It's cold out here. Once you can breathe easily, let's get you into bed. We're both getting soaked." Charlotte's voice trembled. She waited another minute, then asked, "Do you think you can walk with me into the house?"

When he nodded, she slowly guided him inside, dripping water across the hardwood floor as they moved, step by step. She toweled both of them off, helped him into dry pajamas, and put him into bed. His last conscious sensation was the warmth of her body as she spooned him and pulled the duvet around them, not on his side of the bed or hers, but right in the middle.

Andy woke them in the morning, and Charlotte rose to get him off to school. Will dozed off. Later, she returned to the bedroom with coffee. "That was some panic attack you had last night."

"I'm sorry I got you so wet." Will's lip quivered. "I don't know what happened."

"How are you feeling now?" Charlotte searched his face.

"A little shaky, I guess." He rubbed his eyes.

"I think I do know what happened." She gestured for him to sit up and handed him a cup of coffee. "Your body is telling you something important. It needs you to slow down and pay attention to what's happening to you emotionally."

Will took a sip of his coffee but didn't respond for a moment. "I'm scared, Charlotte. I don't know how to deal with what I've done. I don't think I can go through with taking on BioteKem when I've screwed up so badly." His voice trailed to a whisper. "I don't know how to go on. I no longer have a chance to straighten things out with Chet, and I feel like I'm losing you. I know I betrayed you and worry you'll never be able to forgive me."

Charlotte sat next to him on the bed and took his hand. "You scared me last night." Her eyes filled with tears. "You need someone to help you through this. You've been rocked to your core. Yes, you betrayed me, and my own hurt confuses me. I also see that you feel betrayed by Chet. I know you carry the unresolved issues with him as a huge burden. Of course, you're shaky."

Charlotte took a deep breath. "And so am I. I can't help you when I'm as confused as you are. We're a mess." Her wobbly laugh sounded forced. "I need somebody to help me through this, too. I don't know how to deal with my feelings about how you betrayed me. Sometimes I'm so angry I want to kill you, and other days I want to forget any of it happened. Neither is the right way of course." She studied the far wall as she opened her clenched fist.

Will's face went slack. He couldn't remember ever before having a problem he couldn't solve. And, if he did, it was Charlotte who usually helped him solve it. What did their mutual admission mean?

"We need counseling," Charlotte said firmly. "If we want to save 'us' and get beyond the hurt and guilt of betrayal, I think we need a third party to help us navigate through the tough talk about how to get there."

"I'll do whatever it takes." He took her hand and squeezed it.

After a day in bed, Will's body slowly recharged. The weight of his worry about his marriage had shifted when he and Charlotte had agreed counseling was the right path to take. He felt more relaxed than he had in weeks.

That evening, he pulled out Chet's devices, hoping to find nothing new. He expected activity would dwindle as news of Chet's death circulated widely and was anxious to return them to Andrea or ask her what she wanted done with them. IT at BioteKem could wipe them for her, and they could be repurposed to someone.

Thinking back over the past month of Chet's illness and now death, he knew he hadn't shirked any of his duties. He had been driven to meet the moment of the cyberattack crisis while reeling as Chet's last words to him stayed on a repeat cycle in his brain. And now, words Chet spoke to others echoed as well. Chet had never asked him to serve as executor of his will. But Chet's attorney told Amy that he had made a last-minute switch to her the same day he got sick? The day he threatened Will. What was behind that? And how could he face succession talk under these circumstances?

He decided he could move forward only if he did so in small steps. The first was to talk to Larry again tomorrow and report progress on the plans for Chet's funeral. He could also delegate work on the memorial designation plan to PR and Merilee to get started. They could work directly with Andrea on the planning. Now with Amy in the loop he hoped he could ease out of the emissary role for Andrea. He was still emotionally shaken by supporting Andrea just as her husband had thrown him out of his circle of trust. He thought about what would have happened if he hadn't been around for Andrea when Chet needed medical help. The irony of his choice to help was breathtaking; he took a risk in doing so but could never have said no to her. He didn't waste any more of his time thinking about what would have happened if he had refused her request.

He had been working for years to get to the position he was up for at BioteKem, but now that it was within reach, there was no way he could enjoy the next move without solving the mystery of Chet's threat.

CHAPTER 26

First thing Monday morning, Pam Shields asked for a meeting. Fearing he had missed something, he checked BioTechNews for anything new on Bella or her company. Nothing.

"Pam, you wanted to see me. Is everything all right?" Will met her at his office door as she arrived and led her to a chair in the conversation grouping away from his desk.

"Yes, thanks. Everything's good, actually." She sounded upbeat. "We've received a request. The *Boston Globe* would like to do a feature story on you leading up to the transition expected at BioteKem in light of Mr. Sutherland's death."

Will wasn't ready for this. He should have been expecting there would be industry and wider interest in his ascendancy to the top job at BioteKem. "I understand that may be a good thing, but it may be premature. Chet hasn't been gone a week yet." He tried to get ahead of her enthusiasm. "Plans for his funeral and the opportunity to honor him should come first, don't you think?"

"Well . . ."

"I was going to call you about that today. As it happens, I spoke to Andrea Sutherland yesterday and she's interested in directing memorials to one of our scholarship funds. Maybe that could be an angle to start with—highlight Chet, the scholarship fund, and then, at the right time, when the board is ready, yes, then it makes sense for a feature article about the future of the company, and me, as the new leader. If the board chooses me, of course."

"I guess that could work." She started slow, then grasped onto the idea. "We could get more press doing it that way. Good press, so that is smart. Yes, I like it!"

Will knew it was the right thing for the company—and the right thing for him. He swallowed hard. He couldn't put himself in a position to be questioned about the recent article about BioteKem and the SEC. He couldn't imagine how he would field the question, "Are you acquainted with Bella Davis?"

Succession talk and planning couldn't wait for long.

Next, he called Larry for an update. He put the call on speaker so he could walk around the room. "How did it go with calling the SEC?"

"What I expected. They played dumb, at least the first person I talked to. I persisted and expect a call back from a higher-up. I'm hoping I'll hear back today."

Will I ever get a lucky break? Certainly not today. Will pushed his fingers through his hair, his anxiety starting to get to him. He needed to stay cool. "Okay, I see you called earlier. What did you want to talk about?"

"I found Rocco Barletti." Larry blared the good news. "Or I should say I found out where exactly he is, and I think I have a way to communicate with him about our issue."

"Great, tell me more." Will's heart beat faster.

"One of my former associates knows someone who knows him and . . ." Larry chuckled. "Well, I don't want to lose you in the linkages here. Let's just say that I can get a message to him that I need to speak to him."

"What makes you think he will agree to speak to you?"

"That's a bit tricky. I want you to know how I'm thinking of doing it . . . the angle I will use. There's a bit of a risk, but one I believe we should take."

"Go on."

"Well, if I were this Rocco, someone would have already told me about that piece mentioning Met-Med and the SEC rumored investigation. As I'm already a registered investor, actually, I am the only one registered, I've gotta be a little nervous about it."

"I'm following you."

"I'd like to get a message to him that someone who is in contact with the SEC would like to talk to him. A party that has also been mentioned in the article."

"That would be BioteKem?" Will thought he was tracking. "And that would be you, acting for BioteKem, because you've got a call into the SEC?"

"Exactly. You got it!" Larry changed his pace and articulated each of his next words slowly. "The beauty of this—it's true."

Following closely with Larry's every word, Will was so far into Larry's approach he couldn't utter anything other than, "Brilliant."

"Thank you, Will. I thought it was pretty good, too." He laughed aloud, and Will joined him, releasing some of his manic energy.

"Good luck. Let me know how it goes. One last thing. The press is ready to roll on some feature coverage on expected BioteKem leadership changes, but I directed Pam Shields to slow it down a bit. I told her to start with some coverage of Chet, his choice of memorial, etc. all good for BioteKem, before we move on to anything about me."

"Makes sense." Larry's next words could have been Will's. "Yeah, we wanna get done with this other business first."

CHAPTER 27

By noon, things were moving in the right direction. Could that carry over to this mess with the SEC? He hoped so.

He was slogging through when Charlotte called his cell.

"I think I've found the right couples' counselor. She comes highly recommended." Will detected a question in Charlotte's voice.

"Great. Thanks for doing the research. I'm all in. When can we start?"

"She wants to meet with us together first, then maybe each of us separately, and then she'll come up with a plan. She has an unexpected opening for tonight. What do you think?"

"I think we should take it. What time?" Will would do whatever it took to save his marriage and was grateful there was now a process to get there.

He signed off with his usual, "Love you" and to his relief, Charlotte added, "Me, too." Charlotte clicked off, but Will held onto his phone wishing he could hear her sign-off again. As much as he wanted to hear her repeat her words, he cautioned himself not to read much significance in the old habit between them. The last weeks had been a lesson in how two adult parents could keep the pretense of normal going for a long time. He was hopeful pretense didn't get so comfortable it was hard to break.

———————❖———————

Will left BioteKem for a meeting with other industry folks at a nearby life sciences company headquarters to discuss the aftermath of the cyberattack and prevention tactics going forward. Larry, also in attendance, left the meeting for at least twenty minutes to take a call.

After the meeting, Larry pulled Will aside. "Time for a drink?"

Will looked at his watch. "No, I've got to get going, but let's just sit here in the lobby for a minute. Do you have something?"

"I think so." Larry whistled. "But what an adventure to get to this guy. I feel like a character in a John le Carré novel. If I was trying to get to a mountaintop, I would be forced to be blindfolded and then climb up several switchbacks and use code words at each turn." He chuckled. "But I think it was worth it."

"You mean, he was keeping his location a secret?"

"Yes, as well as any phone numbers to his residence or person. I'm sure our conversation was on a burner phone."

"Good God. What could be so worrisome for him?"

"In short, the SEC, and the American court system. He's trying to disentangle himself from anything to do with Met-Med, ASAP."

"Because?"

"Because Met-Med is an empty shell for a company that is selling a nonexistent product. And he was duped to invest in it. He's trying to secure his money."

"How exactly was he duped?"

"By a sweet young thing who sold him a bill of goods." Larry smirked.

"Bella Davis?" Will pushed the words out, recalling the constant sound bite Bella used with any mention of the company Met-Med, in "proof-of-concept testing."

"Yes. By the way, our Ms. Davis was indeed a guest at the mysterious residence of Mr. Barletti, but she was disinvited after his attorneys saw the news report and started doing their own digging." Larry took a breath, getting into the good part of the story. "Actually, he sounded like he had mixed feelings about the decision to send her packing. Evidently, they flew to the Virgin Islands after the conference. He really had no choice. He couldn't afford to get deeper into the legal morass."

"So, what are his attorneys finding out?"

"The company is kaput. Nobody home anymore. We knew that part already, but they are trying to find out if there's any money somewhere to go after, to get his investment back."

"I see. Did they shed any light on the BioteKem angle with the SEC?"

"Not really. I'm hoping to get to talk with one of the attorneys about that tomorrow. Rocco told me they uncovered Bella's MO when going after investors. Seems she's not above using shady tactics to entice vulnerable rich guys into getting what she wants."

"What does that mean, exactly?"

"Don't know. Just that there's a pattern."

Will felt dirtier the longer the conversation went. He remembered a certain titillating intrigue to their hook ups, but he wouldn't characterize them as shady. Could he have been, like Rocco, one of her targets? "Larry, what did you have to do to get this information?"

"Nothing, actually. The guy was ready to talk. Maybe felt relieved to be out of the morass of it. Maybe he just wanted to warn us about Ms. Davis." Larry rubbed his chin.

"I didn't have to bluff at any influence with the SEC I may have been able to exercise. Since you and I both know we have no ability to influence the SEC, I'm happy about that."

Well, that's a win, Will thought. *At least my poor judgment didn't put BioteKem at risk.* However, he was no closer to finding out what Bella had to do with Chet. "As am I. Thanks Larry."

And then, just as Larry was moving to get up, Will asked, "Do we know where Bella Davis is now?"

"No."

Still a missing link.

CHAPTER 28

∎∎∎∎∎∎∎∎∎∎∎∎∎∎∎∎∎∎∎∎∎∎∎

W ill arrived at the therapist's office before Charlotte and walked around the waiting room to calm himself. He noted the educational certificates hanging on the wall for Dr. Betsy Jorgensen, who matriculated at Brown for undergrad and Boston University for her PhD in psychology. He had no context for what to expect from counseling but knew he needed to ace it in order to save his marriage.

Charlotte arrived looking as breezy as he felt taut. In her usual manner of seeing through to his nerves, she gave him an affirming smile and said, "Remember, this is what we both agreed we needed, right?"

He gave her a thumbs-up and smiled back at her as the inner office door opened. Dr. Jorgensen invited them in.

"It's nice to meet you both." She appeared to be in her thirties. Her smile was warm, and her take-charge manner belied her age.

Once they sat, she said, "I'd like to start by debunking a couple of misconceptions about couples' therapy." Her eyes seemed to drill into Will's. "First, sessions are designed not to test you but to help you think about your relationship in ways that may help you. You will assess the value of those lessons yourselves. Most couples experience better value when they trust the process and are willing to be vulnerable with one another. I just help facilitate.

"Second, couples' counseling is most successful when initiated early, before the relationship is beyond the reach of intervention. When it is initiated early on, the success rate is over seventy percent."

Will stared back at Dr. Jorgensen, worried she could read his guilt but happy with the odds. *We will be among the seventy percent.*

Charlotte said, "Makes sense. Thank you."

"With that," Dr. Jorgensen continued, "I'm going to dive right in. My first question is one I need an honest response to from both of you." She focused on each of them individually and asked, "Okay?" Both heads nodded.

"Do you believe your marriage can be repaired? Will, let's start with you."

Will was not prepared for this question; she was moving quickly. He couldn't hide from her. He took a leap. "Yes, I do. I have faith in our love and our history together. I'm the reason our marriage is in trouble, and I am committed to do whatever it takes to repair it."

Charlotte's answer was more tentative. "I wouldn't be here if I didn't think it could be repaired. But we need help in sorting out how."

"Thank you both." Dr. Jorgensen took a note and then turned to Will. "So, you admit to having created a problem in your marriage. Can you tell me about that?"

"Yes, I had an affair. An error in judgment on my part. It's over, and I have apologized to my wife. I feel very guilty and afraid that I've hurt her so badly she will not be able to forgive me."

"Charlotte, do you agree that is the problem in your marriage?"

"Yes, I'm very hurt and sad that Will cheated on me. And confused about how to get through that and move forward." Charlotte teared up a bit when she added, "Somehow, I can't help but think there may have been something lacking in our marriage for the affair to have been an option. It's not just about the fact of it but the why of it."

"Thank you for that insight. Infidelity is not uncommon, but you may take comfort in the fact that most marriages survive the experience." Dr. Jorgensen finally smiled for the first time. "I believe I can help you through this, and we can work together to improve and not just repair your marriage. First, I want to confirm a couple of things before we go ahead and design a process together."

Will exhaled as she verified with both of them that there was no abuse in the household currently.

"Will, can you affirm to me, and to Charlotte, that you are no longer in an emotional or physical relationship with the woman with whom you were having an affair?"

With great effort, Will stopped his mind from overthinking the question. Bella still had a hold on him emotionally. He was trying to rid himself of her—she was still manipulating his life!

"No, I'm not in a relationship with her anymore." He faced Charlotte. "I promised you."

Will slept well that night and went to the office midmorning. While no breakthroughs had occurred at his and Charlotte's first counseling session, he liked Dr. Jorgensen. Even though it was uncomfortable at first, she'd gotten directly into the issues, and he had hopes she would be able to help them.

While he caught up with Merilee, she mentioned she was trying to find out the identity of a mystery woman who had called for Chet, unaware that he had passed away.

Will's antenna alerted him, and he asked a few questions. "She didn't leave a name or say why she was calling?"

"No, just said she had a confidential matter to discuss with Mr. Sutherland and wouldn't speak to anyone else. When I told her that Mr. Sutherland passed away, she sounded shocked and hung up."

"Young, old, any identifiable characteristics to the voice?" Will wanted to rule out his obvious suspect, Bella.

"I'd say mature. Not a youngster. No accent."

"Well, if she calls back, refer her to Larry. Perhaps it's something he can help her with."

"Good idea."

Larry, off-site at an all-day meeting, called Will mid-afternoon.

"The Italian attorney called just now. I thought you'd want to hear right away."

"Yes, I do. What did you find out?"

"It's more like, how much information could I give them. They're desperate to find more investors so that their guy isn't the only one holding the bag, which is dangerous. No one investor would want to be the only party facing the full force of the SEC on an investigation. Mounting a defense alone would be laborious and expensive. I believe they are angling to find any other party that was taken in by Ms. Davis, to join forces in defense, if needed legally."

"You had nothing to give . . ." Will held his breath.

"Exactly. We finally got there, but they started with the opinion that BioteKem was making an investment or going for an ownership stake. They wouldn't tell me why they thought that, but Chet Sutherland's name came up."

"How?"

"I asked and they wouldn't tell me. I specifically asked if Bella Davis had implicated Chet in some way, and they wouldn't confirm it, but they were also careful not to deny it."

"Did you get anything of value from them?"

"I think so. More about the so-called MO that Ms. Davis employed to raise money for Met-Med. Her deal was to target powerful men of a certain age, pull them into her web of mystique—beautiful young woman with a bankable concept—and offer them an early in, a board seat, etc." Larry shuffled a page. "Evidently they have identified a couple of men who fit that pattern and believe they may find more."

"They put Chet in that category?" Will was incredulous.

"Yes, I know it's a tough one to digest." Larry's voice grew weary.

Will was trying to see around the corner of where this was going. "But Chet was nobody's fool. Do you think he would have fallen for that?"

"I'd like to throw it out as ridiculous, but I've seen too much in my career to do that. We have to consider all possible scenarios here." Larry's voice was now more serious. "Think about it. Chet was on his way out and taking a bit longer than many thought he should take for whatever reason—fear of being out of the action, unsure of what he would do next, he has a younger wife, would she want him underfoot?"

Larry waited a moment for a reaction from Will, then continued. "I'm sorry to burst whatever illusions you had about Chet, but it was evident to anyone looking that you were running things and fully capable. More capable than he had ever been. It had to wear on him. I don't think it's too much of a stretch to think he may have been tempted by a young, smart, scientific talent like Bella Davis."

Will listened, but his heart raced. Could Chet have fallen for her trap? Just as he let his mind wander to the possibilities, his stomach roiled. Could she have seduced Chet, as she had seduced him? He stopped himself. He couldn't abide that thought. *It had to have been an appeal to his ego to help her with her company, nothing physical.*

Larry continued, his voice stronger, "This is how it could have played out. She offered him a board spot if Met-Med stayed private, or she angled for BioteKem to make an investment, to bring the company in for sure footing going forward. It could be his valedictory lap—appealing for him. Perhaps Chet was considering which path to take when he got sick."

"Is that what you really think?" Will asked, more sharply than he intended. Here was a clear signal the man who had referred to Will as his honorary son had not been the supportive mentor he'd pretended to be, but really was just one more opportunist with a weak character.

"It doesn't really matter what I think. I need to consider possibilities and to protect the company, which includes protecting the leadership unless or until I know leadership has broken any laws." Larry retained his cool demeanor. "I know there were no laws broken, and there's no evidence that BioteKem or Chet as an executive for BioteKem was on record as an investor or a potential investor."

Will needed to end the call before he let his personal frustration get to him. "Larry," he said, "I apologize for projecting my anger onto you. I do appreciate your views. It's just so disappointing to consider this scenario." He took a breath. "What happens next?"

"Not much, from my perspective. With both the Italian investor and his attorneys confirming they knew nothing incriminating about BioteKem, added to my own earlier internal investigation, I'm thinking this case is closed."

Will couldn't sit still after the call. He needed to cool off. He changed into running gear and headed out to the pathway along the Charles River. His run was intense as he tried to out-pace his thoughts and consider whether the case was really closed. What did that mean, exactly? His relationship with Chet was forever altered. He began to realize he might never know Chet's motivation for wanting to fire him. Now his own shame started him thinking about falling into a trap Bella had set for him. But she hadn't asked for anything. Why not? What were her true motivations?

Will was distracted—even tempted—by the thought Larry considered Chet a weak link. He thought about how perceptions color judgment. He was glad Larry had shared his, and in a perverse way, understood how he could get there. But how could Will live with himself without being straight with Larry? He couldn't. He texted Larry to meet him at a bar they both knew, on his route, not far from where Larry was at his meeting.

Larry arrived first. Will joined him at a corner table and ordered a beer. Larry sat with his legs crossed at the knee, the picture of nonchalance. The man had never appeared sheepish to Will and didn't start now. Without preamble, Will started in a rush before he lost his nerve. "I slept with Bella Davis. But she never asked for any special treatment for her company by BioteKem and never asked for a personal investment from me in exchange for anything. I can open my financials for you if you'd like."

"What?" Larry planted both feet on the floor and leaned toward Will.

"I met her in late January at a conference at Penn. She came on to me and invited me to meet her in New York City in early February. It was about sex. Nothing else. Her hook was that she flattered me and wanted me to mentor me. Said she was impressed with my career track."

"How much time did you actually spend with her? Just the one time?" Larry's voice was steady and low.

"One time in Boston and one night in New York City. In both cases, she said she was in town to meet with potential investors. That's all she ever mentioned about business.

She didn't confide any business dealings to me or ask my opinion about anything. Larry, I was her mark, not Chet. I think Chet may have found out about it."

"Slow down, Will. How would Chet have found out, and why would that matter?"

"I don't know." Will swallowed hard before he admitted the rest. "But there's more. The Friday Chet got sick—that afternoon—he insisted on a face-to-face meeting, off-site, just the two of us. It was a short meeting; fifteen minutes max. Chet was more agitated than I had ever seen him. His words are seared in my memory. He said, 'Chasing tail is adolescent, Will. And chasing tail when offered for a business trade is fatal. And when the product is a fraud, stupid and unforgivable.'"

"Was that all he said?"

"No, not quite. He told me he was going to fire me."

There was silence at the table for a full minute and finally a loud exhale by Larry, who shifted in his chair. "Well, he didn't. If he had any inkling of doing so, I would know about it. There's something you'll want to hear. The SEC phoned me back just fifteen minutes before you called."

Will steeled himself for the worst, but he wasn't even sure what could be worse.

"And?"

"The SEC meeting scheduled with Chet this week was in response to his request. He evidently had something he thought they should investigate."

"Any detail?" Will leaned in.

"No. But, given Chet's death, I prevailed upon them to tell me if there were any open investigations that BioteKem was party to, in order to conclude any question about Chet's request." Larry finished the last of his beer. "There are no investigations that mention BioteKem in any way at this time."

Will stared out the window.

Finally, Larry said. "Did you hear what I said? There are no SEC investigations about BioteKem at this time."

"Yes, I heard you, Larry. I'm just trying to connect the dots."

"Stop trying. As I said this morning, and now can state even more emphatically, this case is closed. There is no SEC investigation, and no further worry about Ms. Davis. That company is in liquidation or will be soon. You can stop worrying."

When Will didn't respond, Larry continued, "Hey, it's not illegal to hook up with an intriguing woman. It's not unheard of for a boss to threaten to fire you, especially if he suspects you have fallen prey to a ruse he avoided himself and wants a good reason to stay at the helm. You have to get past this."

"You think that's what motivated Chet to threaten me?" Will thought about Bella planting the story about the rumored SEC investigation implicating BioteKem.

"Don't know and neither do you. What I do know is that it doesn't matter at all. It's over. Door closed." Larry excused himself with a parting comment. "Let it go, Will."

Will couldn't move. He stayed to finish his beer. *Door closed. Easier for Larry than for me*, he thought. He couldn't turn his mind off but kept flipping the puzzle pieces over in his mind. Is it possible Chet had also been a mark and had refused Bella's overtures of flattery? Had Chet investigated her company and realized it was a sham, then called her out about it? Would that possibly be the scene that Miles Fortney had witnessed between Bella and Chet having lunch? Or is it possible Bella was angry enough to throw Will out into the conversation, saying he was pursuing her and threaten to use that as leverage—buy Met-Med and save your favored son from exposure? Could Chet have been so incensed by the idea he could be blackmailed that he scared her off, called her bluff, and decided to fire Will, thinking he was harming BioteKem?

Any way he looked at it, he felt like a fool. What a colossal failure in judgment to hook up with Bella, who totally played to his weakness. Will had never been a womanizer, never considered himself attractive to women, never knew how to flirt. He remembered how Charlotte had to ask him out for their first date. How had he succumbed to Bella?

He played back Larry's description of her MO—target powerful men of a certain age, pull them into her web of mystique. He didn't fit that demographic. Why had she seduced him? And Chet, if she had targeted him. He was smarter than Will. One of two things could have happened. He was smart enough to investigate her company and knew it was a fraud, or he was manipulated into a vulnerable spot and believed whatever she may have told him about Will. Either way, he would never feel the same about Chet. The worst part was not knowing why Chet wouldn't have given Will the benefit of the doubt and heard him out. They could both have taken this sham artist to task. Instead, they split wide open.

Will would have to live with it. *Not Chet.*

CHAPTER 29

B ack at the office, Merilee had left the draft of the quarterly CEO report to shareholders for him to review. He knew the numbers were down a bit, but that could be easily traced to the supply chain issues related to the cyberattack. The supplies needed to manufacture the biological reagents that BioteKem sold to companies around the world had been subjected to a chokehold due to the fear that Big Pharma would get tangled up in further upstream difficulties. Fortunately, the worst was past, and supplies were starting to flow again. His message to stakeholders needed to be honest, yet hopeful. He made a few slight changes and approved the draft.

Spring was finally coming to April. The evening had a softness to it, the light of dusk spectacular in its hues of gold and coral. Traffic was light due to the hour, and he listened to music on his way home, something he hadn't done for over a month.

He drove into his circular drive guided by the landscape lighting and saw a patch of crocus peeking out of the mulch near the brick walkway. He entered the house.

"I'm home!"

Nobody appeared. He followed the light to Charlotte's office and peeked in from the doorway. She sat at her desk working on the keyboard, scrutinizing what was on her monitor. Computer glasses on and hair pulled up in a bun, his wife was never more beautiful than when she was in her element. He was happy she had a new case to work on, happy she had the diversion from what he had pulled her through this past month. His considerable relief at having couples' counseling gave him more bandwidth to focus on finishing out the mystery. Classical piano music from the sound system filled the room, and he decided to knock lightly on the open door to announce himself and not frighten her.

"Charlotte."

She jumped anyway. "Oh, Will, sorry, didn't hear you come in."

"No worries. Fully involved in your case, I take it?"

"Yes, I'm getting some good traction, so wanted to keep at it." Her eyes returned to her monitor once he nodded.

He left her to her work. He was glad the opportunity didn't present itself to give her an update on the Italian, the SEC, and Chet. Something about it didn't spell closure to him.

After a quick dinner of leftovers, he cleaned up the kitchen before heading up to bed. He stopped in his office and clicked to the online BioTechNews site out of habit. Larry was watching the site now, so he didn't really need to do it. He wished he hadn't.

A new post. Today's date. "Bella Davis has flown back to the United States."

———————— ⬦ ————————

The next morning as she was leaving, Charlotte said, "I forgot to mention this to you last night. Andrea called me yesterday to ask me about that report she wanted to get to the office. Do you remember it? It was right when I was leaving for Florida." Charlotte flushed slightly. "I left it on the dining room table, with a note for you to bring it into Merilee, remember?"

Will clearly remembered that morning. He'd been scrambling to get to the airport for that early flight when he saw the report. "Yes, I do remember, and yes, I did get it to the office."

"I'll let her know. Thanks."

"Any particular reason she's asking?" Will made a mental note to ask Larry about that report, which neither of them had considered a priority back then.

"Don't know exactly. Something about an invoice?"

Charlotte left in a flurry. This time, in her haste, she blew him a kiss, an old habit. "Goodbye."

Her old habit put a bounce in his morning, at least until he arrived at the elevator bank and found Pam waiting to share an elevator ride up to his floor with him.

"Good morning. May I ask where we are with plans for Mr. Sutherland and whether we can start planning the feature article about you?"

"Nothing new since two days ago. The obituary that you helped the family with and the quote you supplied were really nice."

"Good, thanks. We ran it in the business section of the *New York Times*. We used the standard language, noting that a service would be announced soon. Also, I've got a few placements in mind for trade publications announcing the scholarship gift in memorial when we are ready with that."

Will worked to fight his first impulse to squirm. He had to admit Pam was just doing her job, but he'd like a day or two without having to think about Chet and the inevitable board action that needed to follow soon. As they arrived at Will's floor, Pam spoke up again.

"I was wondering if you would be willing to be available for a live event at the school when they receive it?"

"Of course." Will knew this was good for BioteKem, and he was more a champion of STEM than Chet had been.

"Good, I'll check with them." She pulled out her tablet to check the calendar and make a note. "Any idea yet about when the board may meet to take action on succession?"

"Ah, no. I will be discussing it with Larry Weisman as early as today. Not sure when a meeting will be pulled together, but once I know, I'll let you know."

"Great. One last thing. I'm excited about the feature story possibility." Pam stopped walking. "I know this is a little awkward, but I'm sure they'll want photos for the feature, and I'm thinking we should come up with some photos of you that are updated. I've gone through the stock photos we have of you and they're perfectly fine, but just an idea—"

Fortunately, Merilee interrupted them before Will was required to answer. "Your 9:00 a.m. meeting is starting."

I wonder if I look different.

CHAPTER 30

Funeral day arrived. A crisis had been averted when Andrea tapped their community theater as the venue once it become apparent their home church wasn't large enough to handle the expected crowd. Will had been grappling with a dire dilemma of his own since Andrea had asked, "Beyond the religious service, who should be asked to say a few words about Chet—besides you, of course?"

This request had given him a tension headache that had been pulsating for days. How was he supposed to eulogize Chet and not appear disingenuous, when his own emotions about the man were so raw? He had even researched common elements of funeral tributes in an attempt to depersonalize this one to an assignment.

He promised Andrea he would come up with a few people who should be asked to make remarks, hoping he could somehow become less important in the program. He and Merilee pulled together a list of VIPs to consider. But then the events coordinator added Will at the end of the list, in a position befitting the highest-ranking executive at BioteKem.

He had never practiced a speech in front of a mirror until now. The self-imposed pressure to put the past weeks behind him and move forward as the de facto leader caused him to lose sleep and his appetite. Charlotte picked up on his nerves and helped him choose the right tie before they left for the event. Her standard comment, "You'll do fine, Will, you always do," didn't help this time.

As they approached the theater with its marquee, Will thought how appropriate it was that he would be play-acting this final act for Chet. He entered the theater, swallowing hard to tame his stage fright, and with Charlotte at his side, joined Andrea, Danny, and Amy with her kids, Molly and Jay, in the reserved seats in front. Before he sat, he scanned the audience. There were maybe 250–300 people. He recognized most as people from the life sciences community. Many wore suits, but he saw a generational representation of the younger crowd in biotech who had gone casual. Their idea of funeral dress ran to jeans and button-down shirt attire for the men and slacks and jacket for the women.

Andrea pointed out the seats filled with friends and neighbors visiting among themselves in the side section of the theater seating. "The theater folks are over on the other side of us."

Will noted that group as artsy, with jewelry and tattoos proudly displayed, as well as a purple head of hair to accent the group.

Will left his seat to greet the board members personally with a handshake before things got started. He spent the last few minutes before the service chatting quietly with Danny, who appeared ready to faint.

"I'm nervous too, Danny, but we can do this." Will smiled his encouragement and patted the teen's shoulder as the lights were dimmed. Reverend Martin opened the service with a personal welcome and opening hymn.

Following the hymn, Danny read a passage from scripture, halting somewhat and looking to his mother before losing his composure. He closed with, "I'll miss you, Dad." At that, Andrea started to cry, and Amy's eyes welled up as both women welcomed Danny back to sit between them.

More music followed, and then another reading from an actor from the troupe, this time a poem.

Reverend Martin's message was heartfelt. "I had the pleasure of knowing Chet Sutherland for over twenty years. We met when he moved to Waltham and was church shopping. Evidently, my pitch won out." He chuckled and the audience joined him. "We hit it off, and he became a friend as well as a parishioner. I had the honor of officiating at the wedding of Chet and Andrea and baptizing Danny." He stopped and smiled at the family. "It is from a sense of personal loss that I join his family and his community in grieving his departure, too soon."

After his remarks, Reverend Martin introduced three other speakers to "pay tribute to our friend and innovator, Chet Sutherland."

Following the eulogies, a lovely woman in an iridescent dress shimmered onto center stage. With just the slightest accompaniment from the piano, she sang Celine Dion's song, "My Heart Will Go On." The room was soon filled with the sounds of sniffles and swallowed sobs.

Following her song, the songstress walked to the side of the stage where someone handed her a beautiful bouquet of red roses. All eyes remained on her as she walked to Andrea, bestowed a kiss on her cheek, and handed her the flowers.

Will's stomach was a storm throughout the entire funeral, but long experience at staying cool at public events prevailed. He saw the flash of a camera and hoped event security had kept the press out of the theater. Andrea accepted the flowers, lifted her head, and nodded her thanks.

How do I follow this? Up until this moment, Will had been clear about his role as closing speaker. Fill in the blanks, if there were any, and keep it short. All of the relevant remarks had been made giving Chet his due, so he planned to mention things he had learned from him, his gratitude for the mentoring he had generously provided, and skip over any gooey message from the heart.

He climbed the steps to the podium. The auditorium was now silent after the release of emotion evoked by the last song. He scanned the audience before he spoke; his eyes caught something red. Near the door, a woman stood, dressed in black, a black cloche over her hair, her signature red lipstick—Bella. He quickly looked away and held onto the podium to steady his weak knees.

"Friends, colleagues, admirers of Chet Sutherland . . ." He started but was compelled to look again. He snaked his eyes to Bella, but she was not there.

Later, he was told his tribute to his mentor had been gracious and meaningful, hitting the right tone. All he could remember, other than the sight of Bella, was that he had managed to thank people for coming to the funeral and for their support during Chet's short illness and invite them to the reception following at the supper club next door to the theater.

Will left the stage, and the audience started to get up and move toward the doors. As if propelled toward a magic potion he needed to save his life, Will muttered something to Charlotte about going to check with event security to make sure the press was not bombarding the guests and ducked out a side door to get to the front of the building. There were a couple of photographers held back by security, and he managed to squeeze by without notice. The parking lot was packed. He scanned the space for an Uber or taxi pickup, and then the lot itself. His breathing ragged, he finally caught a glimpse of a woman in black just as she was getting in a town car. As she swiveled to get in, the lipstick gave her away. He considered a run to her, but the distance was too great. Instead, he stood and stared at her. They locked eyes only for a second, and where he hoped to see contrition, he found only avarice. Will stood as a statue without a thought about his next step when Larry approached him.

"Nice job on the eulogy." Hearing nothing in response, Larry studied Will closely. "You okay? You look like you've just been hit by a Mack truck."

"Not quite, although I must say it was a shock." Will finally shifted his feet and straightened his back.

"What was a shock?"

Will caught up with his sensibilities enough to realize he sounded a bit crazy. He smiled before he responded. "Bella Davis was here."

"She came to the funeral?" Larry's voice was an octave higher than usual. He couldn't hide his surprise.

"Yes, I saw her in the back when I went to the podium to speak. And now, I just saw her get in a car and drive away." Will straightened his tie.

"What nerve."

Larry's expression was a combination of awe and distaste. Bella evoked more from Will, whose immediate burst of anger was white hot but had cooled just enough for him to direct it. He now recognized her as the enemy she had long been and determined it was time to commit to the best revenge he could mount—by regaining his life.

"Or whatever. We'll have to think about what it means and talk tomorrow. Right now, I've gotta go host this reception." With purpose in his step after having recognized her true motivation, Will finally shirked off the spell that was Bella Davis and walked into his next act like a CEO.

CHAPTER 31

He avoided the throng heading out by reentering through the backstage entrance, rejoined his wife, and took her hand. "Sorry, I didn't mean to leave you that long. Do you mind if we do some mingling on our way over to the reception?"

"No, of course not." She squeezed his hand. "You seem relaxed. Happy that's over?"

"More than you can imagine." Will felt like a balloon that had finally been refilled with life-sustaining oxygen. That interaction with Bella had finally given him the opportunity to see through her artifice to the true core of her being. After all this time being held hostage to her power over him, a split second had broken her hold. Any doubt or lingering empathy was erased. Con artist or failed entrepreneur—he no longer cared which it was. The gall of her continuing efforts at manipulation had to be addressed. He vowed not to allow her to do any more damage. The only question left was whether he would need to declare war.

Together he and Charlotte worked the crowd as they had many times in the past, chatting with business associates. Most of the guests limited their comments to compliments about the service. "A real credit to Chet," as it would be crass to ask Will about his succession at the funeral. One fellow, the former head of a large local health plan, pulled Charlotte aside and whispered, loud enough for Will's ears, "It's your husband's turn now, and he will move BioteKem to the next level. He's already started."

They stayed at the reception until all of the guests had gone and just family remained. Amy and Andrea sat together on a couch in the corner of the room, and the three teens were checking out the remains of the hors d'oeuvres table, chatting quietly. Charlotte crouched down to give the two women a hug. "A sad day but a terrific send-off."

"It was that, yes." Andrea's hoarse voice showed the strain of the day. "I think Chet would have loved it, actually."

Amy, Charlotte, and Will agreed.

Amy added, "Will, thanks to you and BioteKem for making it happen."

"Of course," Will responded. "Chet deserved it." *And now, it's time to move on.*

———◈———

No dreams interrupted Will that night. He slept in and got to the office later than usual. Merilee had pushed back his earlier meetings, and they spent some time reviewing the funeral over a cup of coffee.

"That singer. Wowee! She was amazing. I cried my eyes out during that song," Merilee said. "Who would've thunk it—a funeral in a community theater? But it really worked well, didn't it?"

"Better than I expected, to be honest. And Andrea was delighted."

"You did very well, boss. Your remarks were touching and well received. No surprise there. You always have the right words to say." Merilee rose to get ready for the day's work when she added, with some reluctance. "By the way, Pam would like a few minutes."

"Oh, good." He chuckled. "I'm actually ready for her now that the funeral is over."

"I'll set her up for later, after these first two meetings that I moved back. By the way, I need to have you take a look at this—not sure what to do with it."

Merilee handed him an invoice for $20,000 for services rendered to Chet Sutherland for confidential matters as discussed. What confidential business could Chet possibly have had that warranted such a price tag?

Will read it quickly. "What's this about?"

"No clue. I searched for the name in any accounts payable that we've had for Chet in the past couple of years and didn't find it. I thought maybe you had an idea?"

Will's mind pinged and he repeated the word aloud. "Invoice." He remembered the conversation with Charlotte when she relayed Andrea had asked about the report she had given her to send into the office; she mentioned it was something about an invoice.

"How did we get this?"

"Mrs. Sutherland forwarded it to me with a note that it must be related to some BioteKem business."

"Walk it down to Larry and see if this name . . ." he peered again at the invoice . . . "Stacy James is somehow connected to the report Andrea sent to us around the time Chet was hospitalized. I think it's time we read it."

"Will do."

Merilee left the office with the invoice and ushered in his 10:00 a.m. appointment.

Will didn't think anything more about it until Larry knocked on his door midafternoon and entered before Will could respond.

"We've got a situation." Larry held a thick packet of papers in one hand and a manila envelope in the other.

"That report from a few weeks back—the one we agreed was not a priority—well, it's a priority."

"What is it?" Will couldn't remember Larry quite this unsettled before.

"I think it's a report about that company Met-Med, the Bella Davis company that's on its way to liquidation. It's from a private investigator that Chet must have hired to check it out."

"And?"

"Well, here, you need to read it yourself. It's confusing because the names are redacted mostly, but there was a slip-up once with the company name left intact, so I had to read between the lines."

"Is Bella Davis mentioned in the report?" Will felt his heart thrum.

"No, again, the name is redacted, but how many other people could it be?" Larry started to read from the report. "Stanford PhD Research with J.S. Larsen at UCLA. Scientific advisor and business development in Silicon Valley at NEWWORLD TECH, which developed and commercialized products with direct sales of over $1 billion."

"Okay, okay, it's her." Will grimaced, and Larry handed over the first few pages to Will. He kept the remaining pages for himself and sat to continue to read from where he left off.

Both men read the pages they had, Larry handing over more as he finished every few minutes.

Ten minutes later, when Larry was finished, and Will had read enough, he said, "Let's get Stacy James in here. Looks like we own this report, which means we deserve some answers."

CHAPTER 32

Whether Stacy James was eager to get her money or just motivated to share her story, Will wasn't sure, but as long as she was willing to meet with them the next day, it didn't matter. Larry had also checked her out via his network and had found her to be a legitimate investigator with a good track record.

"She did make one odd request that I didn't explore but managed for her," Larry said. "A reserved parking spot by the elevator."

At the appointed hour, Merilee escorted her into Will's office. Both he and Larry stood as Stacy, a tall woman of about fifty with a sun-kissed face, intense eyes betraying humor at the moment, and her foot in a walking boot, entered the office.

"Gentlemen, thanks for the special parking spot. Ski injury." She approached both men to shake hands, and then Larry pulled up a high-back chair so she could settle in.

"Thanks." She pulled her messenger bag from around one shoulder and set it down beside the chair. "And, before you ask, I wish I could tell you that I made a bad decision and ended up on a black diamond run, but this happened on the way to the lodge when some idiot stepped on my foot with his ski boot still on." She smiled at their expected chuckles.

"Ah, ski trip out West?" Will asked.

"Yes, Vail. I met my kids there for our annual spring break trip. That's why I didn't hear about Chet's death sooner." She placed her hands in her lap. "I was sad to hear the news. I'm sorry for your loss."

"Thank you. He was a good guy and will be missed." Larry pivoted to business. "As I mentioned on the phone, Chet's wife, Andrea, sent us the report you wrote for Chet a few weeks ago, and then forwarded your invoice just this week. But, before we get into that, could you tell us how you knew Chet?"

"Gosh, seems like I've known him forever, but I think we met first when he was affiliated with the Massachusetts Life Sciences Center and I was a business analyst with Pfiffer and Simon, a consulting firm focused on the life sciences. You may know of it?"

Both men nodded. "Are you employed by Pfiffer and Simon now?" Larry asked.

"Oh, no. Haven't been for years. I went out on my own twelve years ago now. I wanted more flexibility to raise my kids, and it's been the right track for me. Most of my clientele are biotech investors looking for the next big product to help launch—something they hope will produce a huge return on their investment. That's what Chet was looking for when he contacted me."

Will asked, "What exactly did Chet ask for?"

"My typical package. Deep background on the principal or founding party of a new company; a review of the basic science behind any product that the company claims will add value to the market; and, if requested, a forensic accounting of the financials to date."

Will shifted in his chair. "I can't help but wonder . . . is it typical to send a confidential report to the client with the name of the company and the founder redacted?"

Stacy laughed aloud. "Oh, my lord. As I started my investigation, there was nothing typical about Chet's request. That's why I pumped the price up so high—Mr. Sutherland kept changing the focus and wanting information from me that I had no way of getting for him." She adjusted her glasses. "He wasn't happy with me when I wouldn't go after it."

"Before we go on, can we confirm that you investigated Bella Davis and her company Met-Med?" Larry asked.

"Yes."

After a few more questions, it was clear Stacy was willing to share all she knew.

"My background check on Bella Davis came up clear. She is who she says she is. The Stanford education and first forays into biotech were validated and successful. Things started going a bit off track for her in the past fifteen months as she has attempted to get this newco off the ground. She's blown through the $2 million she made on her first venture and is desperate to find angel investors to support what appears to be a faulty product, or at least one that has not lived up to the hype."

"So, you interviewed people involved in her first venture, and scientists involved in this testing for Met-Med?"

"Oh, yes. Of course, I couldn't do this work without keeping trust with a network of people in the scientific field. They wouldn't want to be quoted, of course, but that's how I keep them in my network of experts. They tell me the truth." She pulled her shoulders back. "In biotech, the prevailing mantra, 'Fake it till you make it,' is not what my clients expect to guide my work, and it doesn't. In fact, that practice has my business booming. Too many shortcuts taken by too many in the field. I take the long way around to verify what's what for my clients."

Just then Merilee knocked and asked if they would like refreshments. They took a quick break, and when Stacy left to use the restroom, Larry said, "She's clearly got more to tell us. She strikes me as a straight shooter who doesn't play games."

When Stacy returned, she walked past a wall of pictures Will had in his office. "This one of you and Chet looks recent. I take it the BioteKem board will be taking action soon on the CEO position?"

"Yes, that picture is about two years old. Taken just after I came to BioteKem. I enjoyed a good relationship with Chet for over two years. Now that the funeral is over, the board will be taking action soon."

She still gazed at the picture. "He looks good here, much better than the last time I saw him."

"How so?" Will asked.

"Let's just say that I didn't see Chet at his best at our last meeting." She headed to her chair. "I need to sit again. Could I ask you to pour me some coffee and put a cookie on my plate?"

Larry complied with her request, and they all sat again.

"Gentlemen, now that Chet is gone, and the investigation I did for him was ostensibly, at least at the beginning, on behalf of BioteKem, I'm going to be very honest with you about everything that happened. I think it's important you are aware of what went on."

"Thank you. We appreciate your willingness to fill us in on this uncommon situation," Will said.

"Chet was in a real hurry to get my report—a rush job, he said. He was convinced Bella Davis was a genius and anything she touched would turn to market success, so hiring me to investigate was really just the final step he felt he needed before taking action."

"And what action was he going to take?" Will straightened his tie. With a firm link between Chet and Bella, could

Larry's theory that Chet had had a change of heart about retirement be close to what had happened? Could Chet have been planning on pulling in a new company and making a comeback at BioteKem, turning his planned retirement into a joke, and throwing Will out in the process?

Stacy stopped chewing her sweet. "Are you telling me you don't know?"

"Yes, we are telling you we don't know anything about this company or his relationship with Bella Davis. Chet's interest in either or both was not something he discussed with us," Larry said.

"That part of Chet's story was true. He told me he was interested in bringing Met-Med into BioteKem but didn't want anyone to know until he had it sorted out himself, wanted to make a big splash of it, he said." She shifted her tone. "Then I am almost certain he didn't tell you his fall-back plan was to join Met-Med's board as a major investor with Ms. Davis as he retired."

As both Larry and Will stared at her, she went on. "I've already shared the findings of the report itself with you, so you know it was negative, due to the fact there was no viable product. I gave it to Chet, verbally, at his request. He was furious and told me I was wrong."

"Why do you think he reacted that way?" Larry asked her.

"It was obvious to me he was enamored with her, totally head over heels. Like a schoolboy in love. While investigating the company, I found two people who told me Bella Davis was trolling for angel investors among bored older men who wanted to, quote 'stay in the game.' When I told him and called him on his blindness when it came to her, I must have bruised his ego. He got nasty with me; told me I was a bitter divorcee who didn't want anybody to be happy."

"What did you do then?" The anger that she described fit with his own experience when Chet unleashed his anger on him at the boat club. Somehow it made him feel better knowing he was not the only one to be the target of such venom. But he also felt the fool for not knowing any of what might have been going on with Chet's change of personal plans.

"Well, I quit the job, right then and there." Stacy sat up straight and clipped her words. "He thought better of that and asked me to do a deep dive into the financials to vindicate her. When I asked him why the financials were so important to him after all that I had found, he grew so quiet that I acted on a hunch. I asked him if he had sent money to her already. He didn't respond, but I suggested to him that if he had sent her a personal check, he should call his bank and stop payment on it immediately. And then I stood up to leave and told him I'd send him my report."

"Is that the report we have now?" Larry asked.

"If it is the redacted version that was sent to his home address, yes, it should be. He insisted I redact the names of the company and Bella Davis, and that I label it confidential. He didn't want it coming to the office. I refused to arrange a financial accounting for him."

The room was quiet as Will and Larry digested everything they had just heard. Larry, who had been taking notes throughout the meeting, finally put his pen down and said, "You mentioned Chet had asked for information you had no way of getting for him. Can you detail that in any way?"

"Yes, he wanted to know who the men were that had been targeted as angel investors. I told him I didn't know and could not find out. Also, he wanted names of those who had raised doubts about the science behind the metabolic test they were developing. I told him I wouldn't reveal my sources. It seems outrageous in the retelling, but I admit to you both that given his state of mind, I was actually worried he was going to hunt them down. He was so angry that my findings had foiled his plans."

"It sounds like things ended in a contentious manner with him then," Will said.

"You could say that." Stacy finished her coffee. "With Chet, yes."

"Is there something else you want to tell us about any of this?" Larry picked up the crumb she dropped.

"It's not about BioteKem, but you may be interested in knowing that I reported Bella Davis to the SEC for fraudulent claims to investors. I'm a professional and when I find something so wrong, I do the right thing. What Bella Davis was doing is wrong, and if she's still doing it, she should be stopped."

"Well said, Stacy." It was all Will could think to say. This was such unexpected but welcome news he couldn't contain it. He checked Larry's reaction, whose face tilted with the slightest hint of surprise. Will read it as a clear sign of relief, which enhanced his own.

Larry offered a rare compliment. "You are an asset to the biotech community. Thank you for sharing all of this with us."

The three finally stood up and chatted like old friends, now that they had shared such an unsavory story. It was almost as if they needed to move past it together. Will warned Stacy not to take any repeat ski trips in the near term. Ever the businesswoman, Stacy pitched to them that her investigative services were available whenever they needed her. Larry pulled an envelope from his notebook and handed it to her. "For services rendered, Ms. James."

Larry walked Stacy down to her car, and Will took a celebratory walk around his office pondering what just happened. He started to play with the "what ifs" but stopped when he realized he would never know if things would have played out differently if he had read the report earlier or had known earlier that Chet was Bella's mark. His mood was too good to ruin it by going down a rabbit hole. Could they be getting to closure?

Larry rejoined Will in his office and gave him a high five. "Unbelievable," Larry said. "She's astonishing, right?"

"Yes, make sure you find a way to hire her for an investigation sometime soon."

"Absolutely. That degree of professionalism and integrity should be rewarded."

"Speaking of integrity, you may have been circling closer to the truth than I would have dreamed possible with your comments about Chet the other day. I apologize for shutting you down."

"You mean when I painted the possible scenario of Chet as an aging biotech giant who wanted to 'stay in the game' somehow? I was really just shooting darts, but it does seem like I may have been close. Sad, really, to see Chet in that light." Larry picked up his notebook. "This meeting with Stacy took longer than I expected, and I have someone waiting in my office. Let's check in on this tomorrow first thing. I'm going to have to think about this more, consider any angles we haven't looked at yet. Lots to take in."

"Agreed. Let's sleep on all this before we get comfortable that we're finished with it." Will walked Larry to the door and checked his phone, which had been silenced throughout the meeting. A voicemail from Robin Warren.

"Dr. Franklin, thought you'd like to hear this. I got a message from our anonymous source, possibly aka Bella Davis, and I quote, 'How does Chet Sutherland's death relate to BioteKem's interest in Met-Med?'"

Will opened his office door and called Larry back in. "Listen to this," and played the voicemail for Larry. "Doesn't look like we're done with this yet."

CHAPTER 33

W ill punched the address for the dive bar in Brighton into his car navigation system. After the enlightening news from Stacy James on her investigation for Chet, he felt eager to share it with Charlotte and get her perspective. *Just like the old days.* He thought back to their early years together when they shared everything and how effortless it was to stay connected.

After a few sessions in counseling, he was allowing himself to hope they would get back there. Dr. Jorgensen had been clear their situation was not unique. She told them couples who had been married for a long time have a tendency to let go of the activities they enjoyed together that kept their bond strong. Children came; careers took priority. It was not uncommon to drift apart. And a midlife affair by one party in a marriage was not that uncommon and didn't spell the end of the marriage. It served as a warning bell to take steps to reenergize the relationship. Fortunately, he and Charlotte were all in on doing so and came up with their own plan to get things started.

This week, the assignment was for Charlotte to plan a date night.

He smiled when he got her text that morning.

The Last Drop, 6:00 p.m. Beer, Burgers, and Pool.

It had kept him humming all day long. Between the invitation and the Stacy James interview, he was exhilarated by the time he met Charlotte. He also committed to ignore the latest volley from Robin Warren about Bella until morning and enjoy his evening.

Charlotte had snagged a booth in the back, close to the pool table, and was waiting for him. Dressed in jeans and a sweater, with little makeup, her hair tucked behind her ears, she blended into the dive bar crowd. Will registered his city suit and tie. "Oh, God, I should have changed." He kissed her on the cheek and pulled off his tie. "Hello, beautiful!"

She handed him a menu and smiled. "That's a great way to start a date." She glanced at the bar crowd. "You may want to lose the suit coat, also."

They both chuckled.

After they ordered their beer, Charlotte said. "You look pretty happy, how did the meeting with the investigator go?"

"Corny as it may sound, I'm very happy to be on a date with you." He grinned. "Thanks for arranging it. And yes, I'm pleased with how things went with the investigator. I'd love to catch you up, whenever."

"Now, please."

Over their beer, Will shared everything he and Larry learned from Stacy James, with no editorial comments.

Charlotte listened intently until he finished, and the smile on her face started slow but got bigger and bigger until she finally said, "Wow. What started as a really crazy story is beginning to take shape. Good guys and bad guys are finally showing up. I knew they would." Charlotte was still smiling broadly. "Can we order our burgers now?"

"Of course, I'm sorry. We should have ordered earlier." Will hailed a server.

"No worries, I'm just hungry." Charlotte laughed and then leaned toward him, with her serious face. "Thank you for showing me more of the guy I fell in love with, here with me, at this dive bar."

They ordered their burgers, and Will puzzled over what Charlotte meant. "Would you translate that last comment, please?"

"Well, I fell in love with you when you were somewhat naive and unsuspecting of what others' motivations might be. Remember how you underestimated yourself and stayed on the research while others around you took credit for your work and cashed in on what you achieved?"

Will remembered the history but couldn't follow any string of comparison to today. "I remember, but . . ."

"You have developed into an incredible executive talent with a huge heart who can wheel and deal with the best of them. Large-scale strategy is your playground. Even now, after what you've achieved, you still sell yourself short."

"What?"

"All of these weeks since Chet called you out and threatened your job—what were you worried about over that time?" She watched him for a moment. "Not with any possible wrongdoing by Chet. No, you were obsessed with something you may have done that disappointed him, not the other way around."

The food arrived and Charlotte ate a French fry while Will pondered. "Am I right?"

He conceded the point. "You are right. I couldn't imagine what I had done and didn't ever consider what Chet may have gotten himself into." He looked away for a moment to consider how well she knew him, his strengths and weaknesses, and how much he valued her in his life. He stuffed the constant desperation he felt to keep her and smiled. "So, did I hear you say that you are still in love with the guy that I'm showing up as tonight?"

They laughed together, as they had in the old days. Charlotte's eyes twinkled.

"Before I whip you in our game of pool, just one more thought on this crazy story as it is developing. I think it's important." She grabbed another fry and leaned back in the booth. "Why did Bella choose you? Chet fits the MO, as described by the Italian guy and now Stacy James, but you are not, by any stretch, someone to be described as 'a bored guy trying to stay in the game.' You, my love, are in the game, and headed to a bigger job in that game, so why were you ensnared in Bella's trap? I want you to think about that."

Will had been giddy that Stacy had made a report to the SEC about Bella's actions, which had been beyond the pale even in freewheeling biotech circles. But Charlotte's insightful question about Bella's motivation to come on to him pulled him back to reality. He had no illusions about his looks or sophistication with women. He was easy prey for an opportunist like Bella. How had he allowed her to pull him into her orbit at that Penn Conference?

What is wrong with me?

CHAPTER 34

L arry was waiting in Will's office when he arrived the next morning.

"Good morning. You wanted to meet to exchange thoughts on the Stacy James report early." He stood. "Merilee has coffee for us here. A cup?"

"Yes, thanks." Will took the coffee Larry handed to him. "After a good night's sleep, any red flags come up for you?"

"Not at all. I'm still delighted, especially about the SEC report. It was a gift. Now, BioteKem is totally removed from anything to do with Met-Med. As Bella targeted Chet, and nothing ever came to BioteKem, we're not obligated in any way."

"Are we missing anything?" Will asked.

"Nothing obvious. We should discourage that reporter from mentioning Chet's name in that online thread if we can. It's not a showstopper, but it could be a nuisance. I've been thinking about how. Perhaps appeal to her sense of fair play. Why bring in a dead man to the story that will naturally die its own natural death now that the company is close to liquidation?"

"If Robin Warren got that call from Bella Davis, as the anonymous source, what could it mean?" Will asked.

"She's a master manipulator, we do know that. I don't know what she hopes to gain by putting Chet's name out there," Larry said.

They agreed Pam Shields should respond to Warren on Will's behalf with an appeal to kill any thread related to BioteKem and Chet.

"We don't want to raise the stakes on this, just keep it to routine business." Larry then shifted to a more pressing matter. "I think we can move on toward succession now."

Will glanced out the window for a moment before answering. "I know you're ready to get the board process started, but I can't help but feel a bit unsettled still. Give me a day or two?"

"It's a lot to process, I grant you that, but the company will need clarity soon. A day or so is fine, though." As Larry stood to leave, Will preempted any further talk of succession by asking, "There's something that still bothers me. I can't quite sort out why Bella came onto me. What was she after?"

"I don't know. Delving into her motivations is a dead end. We don't know now, and it doesn't really matter. We just need to move forward."

Larry smiled as he left a befuddled Will to finish his morning coffee.

———————◈◈◈———————

Will's reverie concluded with a series of short meetings to complete the morning and early afternoon before he left to announce the memorial gift to the STEM program at Sloane Middle School. While he was finishing his last meeting, Merilee interrupted him to put through an urgent call from Larry.

"What's up now? It's been all of four hours since I saw you."

"Bella Davis wants to talk to me."

"What?"

"That's as much as I know. She left me a message an hour ago that I just saw. Says she got my number from her friend Rocco B., and that we should talk."

"Do you think it's legit?" Will's mind immediately registered danger.

"Don't know, but why would anyone else call and use that name? I should talk to her, just to make sure there's nothing else out there that we don't know."

"Yeah, you're right, I guess."

"I'm ninety percent certain this case is closed, but we don't want to be scheduling a board meeting to discuss your future until we know for sure, right?"

Will felt like he had been thrown into a mountain lake at 30 degrees below zero. *Larry has my back, right?* "Yes, you're absolutely right. I'm leaving the office shortly but will be back late in the day. Can you meet me here later?"

"Yes, assuming I can reach her at the number she gave me. I'll come to the office when I can," Larry said. "Don't worry."

Don't worry? This was proof Will's intuition not to rush to succession had been spot-on. Whenever Bella Davis was involved in his world, it made for a wild ride. He was glad to have the pleasant distraction of an outing for the next couple of hours.

Will always enjoyed visits to the school to see the progress on the STEM program. He immersed himself in the milieu of excited kids and future possibilities for them, and he and Andrea handed over a generous memorial gift in Chet's name. As they were leaving, Pam Shields, who had been there to record the gift-giving, pulled Will aside. "These pictures of you are just what I was hoping for to add a dimension beyond the more business-related ones we have. This whole program will be great for the feature article that will run soon."

There it was again. The inevitable march toward succession.

CHAPTER 35

I t was after 6:00 p.m. when Will returned to the office. Larry had texted him to say he would join him shortly.

When Larry arrived, Will studied his face closely to get a clue about how things went with Bella, but he was inscrutable. "Tell me about the call. I just want the drama to end."

"Well, it turned out to be an in-person meet. Surprised me. We met around the corner at the coffee shop. She's a very attractive, almost magnetic personality. I understand how people could fall under her spell."

Will felt oddly pleased Larry had experienced Bella's appeal. But he hoped Larry hadn't been taken in.

Larry walked Will through the meeting. "She was a bit coy before getting to the point of our meeting. She complimented me on taking a chance in agreeing to meet and established my position at BioteKem and my relationship with Chet. Finally, she offered a trail of crumbs that I followed, one at a time."

———⟨⟩———

"Rocco tells me that he had a nice talk with you, and that you talked with his attorney, as well," Bella began.

"Yes, I did," Larry replied.

"You discussed the SEC?"

"Yes. Mr. Barletti's attorney mentioned Chet Sutherland in our talk. Why did you want to talk to me, Ms. Davis?"

"I'd like to exchange information with you, if you are willing to enter into an agreement with me."

"What type of information?"

"About my relationship with Chet Sutherland."

"I have no interest in any type of personal relationship you may have had with Mr. Sutherland."

"You do have an interest in any type of relationship that may have led to a violation of the SEC rules, correct?" Bella persisted.

"Was there one?"

"If there was, would you be willing to make an agreement to make sure it would never be disclosed?"

"I'd have to be convinced there was something material that would harm the company if it became known."

"Good. I hoped we could do business together, Mr. Weisman. I believe you are smarter than Mr. Sutherland."

———⟨⟨◇⟩⟩———

Larry summarized the rest of the conversation. "She relayed the same story we heard from Stacy James. Chet was considering pitching a total purchase of Met-Med to BioteKem and staying on as CEO, or if that didn't look likely, he was going to make a personal investment in her company and become a board member. But he suddenly declined, with no explanation." Larry slowed to allow Will to process this before continuing. "Here's where Stacy's story ends, but Bella's gets interesting. When Chet cooled on her business proposition, she pulled something else out of her bag of tricks. She told him she had a sexual relationship with you and that she was sure you would be interested in an investment opportunity once you were CEO of BioteKem."

Will almost leapt out of his chair. "What?"

"Hold on. It's the answer to why she came on to you. She needed an insurance policy and was prepared to bully Chet into a deal. She said Chet went ballistic when she mentioned you. He evidently called her nasty names, names she wouldn't repeat to me. She said, in her own understated style, 'He didn't understand it was just a business arrangement. I believe he was about to report me to the SEC when he got sick.'"

Larry exhaled loudly. "She's a trip, that woman. Totally cold and calculating through this whole episode of Chet's passing." Larry moved his weight forward to lean closer to Will before he continued.

"She told me, in the spirit of full disclosure, she's in the process of liquidating her company and returning any money she received from investors, including Rocco's. She's ready to move on to other ventures and wants to start with a clean slate. Finally, she got to the ask. She wants to make sure there's no SEC report from BioteKem in the works."

Larry leaned back in his chair before he continued, "I basically stayed quiet and made her lay out why she thought I would be interested in any deal. Eventually, she stated it clearly. 'Isn't Will Franklin about to be named CEO of BioteKem? Do you want it out there that Will had an affair with me in return for a favorable consideration for an investment in my company?' When I mentioned she was in liquidation, she said, 'You may have a SEC report in the works about my company. I'd like your assurance that there will be no report, and then, there will be no rumor out there about Will Franklin. Seems fair to me. You?'"

As Larry spoke, Will paced around the office, stone-faced but swallowing a scream. When Larry finished, Will sat down and pounded the table with his fist. "She's unbelievable. Nothing more than a con artist and a blackmailer. She can't get away with it!"

Larry sat patiently, allowing Will to vent his anger. Will finally said, "What do we do?"

"Nothing."

"What? You can't be serious." Will jumped out of his chair.

"Bella is asking for us to stop an SEC report. We never made one, Chet never made one. We have no grounds to make one. Stacy James made one, but Bella doesn't know that. End of story. Yes, she's a master manipulator, and we will never have anything to do with her, but through no action on our part, she believes we have met her request."

"That can't be right. She's got to be stopped."

"From what? She won't be peddling the rumor about you. It harms her as much as it harms you. She's done with us. She's giving the investors back their money. There is no foul play here, just a big stink, but she has cured her faults and is moving on."

Will considered Larry's words while taking one more lap around his office, then pulled out his supply of bourbon and poured them each a drink. His ego, his pride, his belief in his own judgment was so wounded, he was scarcely able to speak. His relationship with Chet had been a lie, his fling with Bella a major mistake. Finally, he poured out these feelings to Larry over the next thirty minutes.

"Chet was like a father figure to me . . ."

Larry sipped his drink and listened. Together they pieced it together. Larry offered his theory that Chet must have gone crazy when he had been bested by Will, whom he considered a young rival for Bella's attentions.

"Once Bella mentioned you, he must have turned on her. That's probably when he contacted the SEC for a meeting. The good thing for us is that she doesn't know he didn't get very far with it. She has no idea about Stacy James and what type of investigation Stacy did for Chet. She doesn't know that the results of the investigation led Chet to stop any forward movement on a business relationship with her, and she clearly doesn't know that Stacy, as a professional in the business, made an independent report to the SEC."

"So, that's what led to Chet threatening my job?"

"That's my bet. It must have been hard losing out to you, especially after Stacy confirmed he was having second thoughts about giving up his power at BioteKem. He then saw you as his rival. He was finished, and you were just beginning."

Finally, Larry stood, as unruffled as Will was undone. "You've had a hard life lesson here. However, hard lessons are valuable at times. Take a day or two to think this through. I'm sure you will see it my way."

"How did you leave it with Bella?" Will was hollowed out.

"Oh, I finished it." Larry went on to explain he ended the standoff by telling Bella the truth. BioteKem was not making a report to the SEC and had no interest in the personal lives of its executives. Larry rose from his chair and picked up his glass. "It was the strangest thing. She played a game of cat and mouse with me throughout the meeting, but finally, I saw her show a bit of emotion, and I had to look carefully. Her shoulders dropped an inch, and I noticed a glimmer of a smile as her brow relaxed. It was as if she just wiped her hands of a sticky issue—and then after the briefest of goodbyes, she walked away, head held high."

It took a minute for Will to take Larry's words in, but when Larry held out his glass, Will rose and lifted his glass, as both drank their last sip of bourbon.

"Tomorrow is a new day, Will. Embrace it. Good night." Larry walked out the door and closed it, as unruffled as when he had entered.

CHAPTER 36

He finished it? Will drove home slowly, considering Larry's words. He knew it would never really be finished. He would live with the stain on his character forever, even if only he, Larry, and Charlotte knew about it. He knew that when he had succumbed to the charms of a con artist, he had inadvertently become the tool Bella used to up the stakes of her intimidation game with Chet. He would never really know what had set Chet on a course to upset his plans to retire and throw Will out. How and when had Chet changed from a man who described Will as the son he wished he had to the bewitched old man who was scheming to fire him?

He drove onto his block, and as he neared his house, he noticed every light in the house seemed to be on, including the outdoor lights.

"Damn, book club night."

Charlotte had reminded him that morning it was her hosting night. The joke among all of the book club members was there must be an unwritten code among husbands not to interrupt a meeting. Spouses were either absent from sight during the meeting or seen only for a quick hello.

It was now 9:00 p.m. Will assumed they would be meeting until around 10:00 p.m. His choices were to either leave for an hour or duck in and wave quickly as he went for the stairs. Cars were parked in the circular drive, blocking his way into the garage, so he parked down the block and came through the garage door into the back of the house. He almost made it to the stairs when Dana, a member, saw him and gave him a secret wave and smiled at him as he made it to the corner, slinking up the stairs. He had a few minutes to chat with Andy before his lights out, and then, his body surrendered to the effects of bourbon on nervous exhaustion, and he quickly fell asleep.

The next morning, after Andy's school pickup, Will joined Charlotte in the kitchen where she was handwashing wine glasses from the night before.

"I saw you try to sneak by the group last night." Charlotte laughed lightly. "Dana whispered to me after she saw you, and of course she took the opportunity to ask when you would be named CEO." She raised her eyebrows. "You got home late. Everything okay?"

"About that. There's some more to the story." He sat on a barstool across from the sink with a cup of coffee. "Bella asked for a meeting with Larry. Wanted a deal."

"What type of deal?"

"BioteKem wouldn't report her to the SEC, and she wouldn't spread the rumor about her . . ." Will searched for a word choice to describe his betrayal of his wife.

Charlotte, carefully placing a wine glass on a towel to dry filled in the gap. "Fling with you?"

Will nodded and relayed the details from the meeting, concluding with Larry's assessment that it was done.

Charlotte had finished washing the wine glasses but stood by the sink facing her husband. "Wow, amazing rivalry motivation by Chet. I didn't see that one coming.

Tell me again. What was it he said to you that Friday afternoon, exactly?"

Will recited the words, now a common refrain. "'Chasing tail is adolescent, Will. And chasing tail when offered for a business trade is fatal. And when the product is a fraud, stupid and unforgivable.'"

Charlotte's face brightened, and she pressed her hands on the countertop. "That's it. God, how cornered he must have felt." Her voice softened. "I think he was describing himself, Will. He probably couldn't admit it to himself, so he projected it onto you, his heir apparent."

Will hadn't considered this. Did Chet really have to project the worst onto him to live with his decision to outdo a rival by framing Will based on Bella's unscrupulous lies?

"It's all so sad." Will's head fell.

"Yes, it is, but hopefully the story is almost over. I agree with Larry on that." Charlotte reached across the counter to lift Will's chin and raised her voice. "I'm well into my journey of forgiveness for your transgression with that awful woman, but—"

Will jumped from his stool and pulled his wife to him. He trembled with anger and held her close until both of them had calmed.

Charlotte pulled away gently and whispered, "Can we please end this chapter and move on?"

"Yes, of course. There's nothing I want more. We'll talk again later." He kissed her forehead and left for the off-site conference he was scheduled to attend.

Will knew he would face lots of questions about his immediate future at the Life Sciences Summit, an annual conference to encourage young scientists to carve out a career in the life sciences. As he scanned the crowd, he saw many of the same faces here as he had ten days ago at Chet Sutherland's funeral. His stock answer, "Yes, I believe the board will be taking up the matter soon" was becoming stale, even to himself. He needed to stake a claim on his future, risks and all, or decide to duck out of BioteKem completely. This he knew. But right now, he was a panelist here to motivate the ambitious talent of the day.

"Dr. Franklin, you are now the highest-ranking exec at BioteKem, you have a PHD in microbiology, and at least two biologic agents to your credit as a researcher. Could you please speak to us about your career track?"

Will stood at the podium facing the audience of three hundred students in the life sciences and spoke from the heart. He explained how he had started out as a scientist intent on finding ways to ease human pain and suffering. He had been a research nerd in a lab when he met his future wife, Charlotte, who saw in him a leadership quality that she thought he should use to accelerate scientific findings into the market, to help people. He admitted he had to work hard not to lose sight of the end goal while learning to navigate the competitive landscape of Big Pharma and biotech. He explained he kept the passion of his end goals in mind by staying current on R&D at BioteKem and how, with an eye toward the future, he was investing in STEM education by sharing his own talents and resources.

As he listened to the other panelists, he continued to review his own life lessons. Will had learned to be wary of traps, false friendships, the temptations of others that shaped his choices, and careful who he trusted, Charlotte being his most trusted since the day they met. He also had learned that while his moral compass had failed him in his weakness with Bella, it had been sorely tested and found to be intact with his caring for Chet's family. That same compass was intact when he led his own company and many others, to stabilize their workflow during and after a cyber-attack that could have brought the industry down.

The hard lesson was Chet was human, and so was Will. Even good people made mistakes. He was going to have to live with that. He could either fall victim to his weakness and self-doubt or incorporate the lesson into his life to make better choices for himself and his family. He knew how lucky he was. He knew this newfound insight, supplemented by Charlotte's wisdom, should inform his next steps.

Larry came by the following morning, with his corporate lawyer demeanor intact. "Good morning, Dr. Franklin. How are you today?"

"Good. You?" Will noted the formal but pleasant banter with Larry and wondered what it meant. He gestured for Larry to pull up a chair near his desk, where just two days ago they emptied their bourbon glasses together.

"Do you have any time on your calendar this Friday morning?" Larry asked, still serious.

"I do, yes."

"Excellent. Then it is my honor to request your presence at a special meeting of the BioteKem Board for the purpose of appointing you CEO of the company."

Will broke the tension first, with a tentative grin, followed by a broad, full-face smile by Larry. Will, exhilarated after a moment of suspense, guffawed. "You had me going there for a moment."

"Yeah, I was hoping I would. Just to keep life interesting."

Larry started to chuckle, and Will joined him—no words necessary to explain their shared relief or newly strengthened bond.

Merilee was quick to enter Will's office as Larry left, with a wink as he passed her. "We have a board meeting this Friday, I understand."

Will stood and straightened. He knew now there was no age limit to personal growth, and perhaps his character had finally been forged in the last month. He was now ready to take the helm of BioteKem and lead it with humility and as a servant to the greater social good. He was grateful Larry had kept a cool head, handled the business with Bella, and advised Will to take a day or two to process and pack it away.

Even now, with Larry's help in managing the timing of board support, Will had to fight off a bit of imposter syndrome in accepting the promotion. But Larry had reminded him he had been doing the job for almost three years, with Chet not in evidence for the last twenty-four months.

"It's your job. Go and get it."

Finally, he was ready. *I can do this.*

CHAPTER 37

After early morning traffic was over, he left the house dressed in the suit and tie Charlotte picked out for him. A different man might have felt cheated or disappointed that there was no fanfare to go along with this appointment. Perhaps the Will of a year ago might have thought he deserved a grander event than the low-key affair board leadership considered appropriate less than two weeks after Chet's funeral. But not this Will.

The vice chair of the board, Carter MacNamara, opened the meeting with a moment of silence for Chet, and then, having been briefed by Will, gave the board an update on the family's situation, and the scholarship memorial granted in Chet's name. There were a few comments about how lovely the funeral service was and how they would all miss Chet.

Next, Carter commented he had been devastated to learn of Chet's death, and it would take all of them time to grieve. The company had positioned itself well for succession, and while it required board action, it wasn't envisioned to happen in this way.

"I know we will have a chance to mark this occasion in a more festive way at some point in the future." He then asked Larry to outline the governance duties ahead of them.

Larry was the statesman and guide for them, and his steady manner at this moment was appreciated.

A few board members spoke on Will's behalf. Then a letter from a competitor was read aloud recounting Will's efforts to get many named companies aligned in an effort to leverage their supply chains to replenish quickly diminished materials during the cyberattack, calling him "a man of the moment." Carter followed with a note from Andrea Sutherland about Will and Charlotte's care for her and her son during Chet's time in the hospital: "Will took care of us when we weren't even sure what we needed. He was always there for us."

Will, more comfortable in heaping praise than receiving it, pinched his thigh to control his emotions.

Finally, Robert Hawkiss, chair of the search committee when Will was recruited, who had been quiet for much of the meeting, asked to be recognized.

"Will, you have been acting as CEO for some time, and we all know it. Today, it is my honor and privilege to make if official. I move to appoint Will Franklin as CEO."

Will asked a point of order about whether he should leave the meeting and was told they wanted him to stay. It was a unanimous vote.

Carter MacNamara asked, "Could everyone lift their glass or coffee cup, or whatever you have close by to toast Will Franklin, our new CEO."

As per their routine, Carter then asked Will to give the board a short briefing on current business before they adjourned.

Will mingled with the board members over a light lunch in the adjoining lounge and accepted congratulations from all of them.

"High time for this, Will. Even under these circumstances, it feels like a long-awaited and celebratory moment. Enjoy it!" Carter McNamara enthused.

"Thanks, Carter." Will smiled.

Time to focus on the future. Finally.

The executive team joined them for the toast of midday champagne and cake, and light laughter and jovial conversation carried on for the next hour. Will stepped out for a moment to text Charlotte.

Unanimous support. It's official. I love you.

Once the room cleared, Larry approached him with congratulations.

Will said, "I didn't expect it to be quite that easy. It was you, Larry. The group was in good humor because they were so grateful that this most important of governance duties was pulled off so smoothly. You are a master. Thanks . . . for everything."

"Hey, never forget. You are the one who performed. You are the one who should lead this company. It's you who got this job, and nobody handed it to you. Don't ever forget that."

How can I ever forget anything that happened this past month?

CHAPTER 38

P am Shields had been waiting for the meeting to finish up. She stopped by to set up the technology for the prearranged interview with the journalist who was ready with the feature article and just needed a few minutes to interview Will before it went to press.

"He's shared with me his outline and much of the article in draft, which is very good. He'll be looking for quotes about where you want to take the company in the future. Also, how you decided to take a risky leadership position with your competitors to share materials across your own supply chains to keep customers from experiencing damaging medication shortages."

She stayed in his office with him as the journalist interviewed him on a video call.

Will knew this moment in time was newsworthy for biotech. Industry watchers were waiting for an announcement after Chet's untimely death. *Time to move into CEO mode.* He expressed his optimism about the company's future, how excited he was to lead it, and detailed new initiatives in the works. "This recent speed bump of the cyberattack was a message for all of us, but leveraging our resources to smooth out the supply chain was just the right thing to do for the country. This may be an odd comment coming from me, but sometimes profit is a secondary factor."

Will drove home just before dusk. The red bud trees were beginning to flower, and rain was more likely than snow to fall. It could be a beautiful spring. His worries about more surprises ahead faded with every passing hour. He thought about his interview with the journalist. What he hadn't told the journalist, but what was most true, was that he and Charlotte had worked together on sorting out every new opportunity, each of the overseas moves, and knew what the BioteKem opportunity would provide for Will in his desire to make a global impact.

He turned into the circle drive and found balloons and twinkly lights outlining the front door. He loosened his tie and headed into a party. His party. Charlotte and Andy wore party hats and greeted him at the entry.

"Congratulations, Dad!" Andy shouted.

Will hugged each of them. Charlotte asked him to give them a report on the events of the day, which he did.

"Look what arrived for you today!" A large spray of spring flowers graced the dining room table. She handed him the note.

Will, it's about time! We're on your team now and in the future.

BioteKem Senior Executive Team

Will looked up at Charlotte. "Merilee arranged this, right?" Charlotte smiled. "Of course, she did."

For the first time in weeks, family took priority that weekend. Will and Andy played catch in the driveway, and all three of them took a drive out of town to do something new—birdwatching along the coast, toward the Cape Cod National Seashore. Will's father had been an avid bird-watcher, and he remembered some fun outings with him trudging along with binoculars. His dad had been a true nerd about it, obsessed about logging every sighting and working on his lists, even planning vacations with a possible bird in mind. He thought about what passion he would pass onto his children. Passion for work? Is that how he wanted to be remembered?

No way. Time to pivot to family first.

Overall, it was a successful day, with sand in the shoes and a couple of birds identified with the help of the bird book Will found in his bookshelf. A rare fast-food drive-in meal topped it off.

"I would do this again, Dad. It wasn't as bad as I expected. Maybe we could get another pair of binoculars?" Andy asked.

When the Sunday paper arrived, Will's heartbeat quickened. As he searched for the business section, his shoulders released their tension and his pulse slowed when he read the feature article. He handed it to Charlotte.

"It's really quite good."

It began with laudatory comments about Chet for his contributions, the generous memorial that was started in his name, and the natural sequence of the BioteKem board elevating long-recognized successor Will Franklin to the CEO role. Will's expected visit to Washington the next week to brief a Homeland Security congressional committee was mentioned. There was even a brief summary of the work Will had led to guide the biotech companies through the supply chain and customer service issues brought on by the recent cyberattack. The "man of the moment" quote made it into the article.

Tish made a video call home Sunday to congratulate her dad on the newspaper article. She commented about the photo of him and Charlotte elegantly dressed at a BioteKem gala a year before.

"You two look all glammed up in that photo. Nice!"

———————⟨⟩———————

Monday arrived, and Will went into the office for a few hours before flying to DC with Larry for the scheduled appearance before the congressional panel. Late morning, Merilee brought him the morning's mail so that he could see some of the early congratulatory cards before he left.

Somehow, he detected it before he even opened it—a handwritten envelope addressed to "Will." No address. It must have been delivered in person.

Congratulations, Will. I hope you can forgive me.
B

He read the note twice. *Forgive her? She's got to be kidding!* The sheer audacity of what Bella was prepared to do had shaken him, but it was time to move on. He rolled his eyes and pushed Bella out of his head space completely, shredding the note into tiny pieces and depositing it in the recycling bin near the case that held Chet's devices, ready to be wiped clean.

CHAPTER 39

One week later, Will whistled a happy tune as he carried the last bag downstairs to place with the other outbound luggage arranged by the front door. Oliver's arrival the night before to help them with Andy for a few days ushered in a busy weekend. He looked fondly at his son and father-in-law ensconced on the couch playing a game of chess.

"Ollie, you're the only one around who could distract Andy from his video games to play a game of chess."

"He's getting better, too. Every time I see him, he gets closer to beating me." Ollie responded with a laugh.

"Grandpa, this time I will beat you," Andy said with bravado, while considering his next move.

The doorbell rang, and all three of them looked to the door.

"Expecting someone?" Ollie asked.

"Nope." Will checked his watch. Too early for the Uber to be here. He opened the door to Andrea Sutherland. "Ahh, what a nice surprise."

"I hope I'm not interrupting anything." Once she noticed the luggage arranged by the door and then the game-playing duo, she said, "Oh, and you have company. I'm so sorry, I never just drop in on people—"

"Andrea, it's okay. Let me introduce you." He guided her into the next room. "I'd like you to meet Charlotte's father, my father-in-law, Oliver Sperry."

Oliver stood and, with outstretched hand, said, "Nice to meet you, Andrea. I'm sorry for your recent loss." He held onto her hand for a moment. "I know how hard it is to lose a spouse."

Will watched his father-in-law's gentle manner with Andrea and was reminded how much Ollie still missed his wife, gone now for several years.

Charlotte appeared from the kitchen with a towel thrown over her shoulder. "Did I hear Andrea's voice out here?" Charlotte hugged her friend. "You have privileges with us to make a drop-in visit. That's what friends do now and then."

"Well, it looks like you're on your way . . ." Andrea pointed to the luggage. "Where are you off to?"

"I don't really know! Will says it's a surprise. All he would tell me is that I'll need hiking boots but no passport." Charlotte laughed.

"Mom, Grandpa knows. He'd probably tell you if you asked him nicely."

"But I'm not going to ask. A surprise is just fine right now." Charlotte smiled back to Andrea.

"Will and I are going on a short trip, a getaway of sorts." She smiled over at her husband. "Do you know we haven't been away together, alone, on a trip that wasn't designed around a business commitment for eons. Actually, we can't even remember the last time."

"It's a head scratcher. Fortunately, the timing was right now. It's been a tough several weeks." Will smiled gently at Andrea. "For all of us." Will's empathy for Andrea was palpable. Protecting her from more emotional distress was high on his list of priorities. He also had his own family to

protect and his marriage to repair. This trip, his date assignment, was an important step on the journey back to full trust
that Charlotte, in her generosity, had allowed them to take.

"Dad accepted our invitation to stay with Andy while we
take a short trip," Charlotte said. "How are you, anyway?
Is everything okay?"

"Ah yes, just taking things slow and easy. Day by day
seems to be best right now." Andrea glanced again at the
luggage. "I do think Danny and I will start thinking of some
travel at the end of the school year, just to have a new adventure, try to . . ." Her voice dropped off.

Will rescued her. "A great idea. Something to look forward to and make some new memories."

Andrea nodded and then regained her focus. "I did drop
by for a reason," she said, laughing lightly. "It's about Chet's
car. I've decided to give it to Jay. Amy agreed it would be
okay. It's good for a young man to have a car." She was
rambling. "I'm driving it over to their house now."

"That's generous of you," Will said. "I'm sure he'll be
glad to get it."

"Anyway, when I was cleaning out the car this morning,
I came across this." Andrea pulled a phone out of her jacket
pocket. "It must be Chet's. I didn't know he had another
phone—it's not on his regular service plan."

Will's eyes met Charlotte's after both had first landed
on Andrea.

"It's dead, of course, and I didn't find a charger with
it." Andrea went on as if she was still trying to solve this
mystery. "I'm thinking of just adding this to the devices that
I gave you before—for any business tracking you needed to
do. I think you've now taken them into BioteKem for—what
is it that happens—wiping?"

"Yes, that's right. They do something magical to clear
all of the data and files on a device so it can be re-purposed

for someone else's use." Will knew what may be on the phone and didn't want Andrea's curiosity aroused. He was still in protective mode with her and learning of a relationship between her husband and Bella at this point would be painful. "I can certainly take care of that for you, if that is what you'd like me to do."

"Yes." Andrea seemed to follow his offer as confirmation of her own idea. "Yes, that's what I'd like you to do." She handed him the phone. "Thank you, again, for helping me out."

"Of course. Happy to do it." Will soothed himself as well as Andrea.

Charlotte changed the conversation to a happier subject. "Does Jay know about the car or just Amy?"

Andrea's face brightened. "That's the fun part of today. Jay's home from school this weekend. It will be a huge surprise for him. Amy planned it this way. Then, Amy, Jay and Molly will drive it over to join Danny and me for dinner out tonight!"

"Oh, how fun!" Charlotte laughed, then put her arm around Andrea and added, "What a nice thing for Jay to have something of his grandfather's. So thoughtful of you."

"Yes, I wish they had had some time to become better acquainted, but I thought this was something I could do. But now, I need to get going, and you two need to get on to your adventure!"

"The next time Tish is home, we should plan a family dinner for all of us," Charlotte said, and Will added, "Yes, let's do that!"

Charlotte walked Andrea out to the car to see her off and when she returned to the house, she joined Will to stare at the phone he had now placed on the kitchen counter. Will said what they were both thinking.

"It's probably the phone Chet used for his conversations with Stacy and Bella. Maybe others." Will stated the obvious but waited for Charlotte's response.

Charlotte added, "And by giving it to you, Andrea has signaled she doesn't want to know about any of it. Nothing about any possible dalliance beyond her marriage with Chet. She wants that chapter closed." She searched her husband's face and squeezed his shoulder. "As do we all."

Will left momentarily and returned five minutes later, whistling again, a padded mailer in his hands, addressed to Larry Weisman at BioteKem. He tucked the phone in the envelope and sealed it tightly, then held it up to show his wife. "Ollie, could you please mail this early in the week? The post office is only a couple of blocks from Andy's school."

"Sure, piece of cake. It will give me a destination in my wanderings around the neighborhood." Ollie mugged at his son-in-law, while his daughter beamed up at her husband.

"So, that's done!" Will kissed his wife on the cheek, thanked his father-in-law, and went to chat with Andy before taking off.

With all preparations made, he took a moment to fully acknowledge the chaos of the last several weeks and how he was now beyond it, fully embracing the lightness in his core being. As if the universe had finally given him permission to move forward. Even the test of a new surprise, the sudden appearance of the additional phone they had surmised Chet had used for betrayal, hadn't rocked him the way it might have in the not-too-distant past.

It had taken him time to adjust to the peace of it. Even through the board meeting approving his CEO position, he harbored the worry that something would occur, a telegram received, an alert on someone's phone, an unexpected shareholder demanding entrance to the meeting—someone calling him out as an impostor or guilty party in a securities fraud. Perhaps it was all unnecessary worry, but still he considered it possible that any number of things could appear and destroy his career, as engineered by Bella.

Today, he chose to leave the puzzle of Chet and Bella behind him and claim the right to his future with neither of them crowding his thoughts. The couple's counseling that he and Charlotte attended reminded him of the solid foundation his marriage could be again. He worked at it, and the glimmers of light he saw in his wife's eyes were his reward.

As they waved goodbye to Andy and Ollie, Will stepped lively into his future, Charlotte by his side.

ACKNOWLEDGMENTS

This work of fiction came together against a backdrop of pandemic recovery and a seemingly unending series of moral challenges in our collective world. My writing is character driven, and it fits that ambiguity and betrayal set the stage for *Behind the Lies*, my first mystery.

Many thanks to the talented staff at She Writes Press for their guidance and support during my publishing journey, which has now resulted in three novels. Brooke Warner's vision and focus on excellence permeates the press. Special thanks to Shannon Green for patiently keeping me on track and Tabitha Lahr for her beautiful design instincts, which brought my pages to life.

Thank you to Annie Tucker, my editor, for helping me embrace the elements of suspense and tension that brought this mystery into full flower. What a fun process to make the pivot with you!

Finally, thanks to my loyal readers and growing author community, who together keep the faith with me as I find my way. It takes all of you, and I appreciate the company!

ABOUT THE AUTHOR

Author photo © Leslie Plesser

MAREN COOPER grew up in the Midwest and now resides in Minnesota. She currently serves as a volunteer for various non-profits and retreats frequently to the shore of Lake Superior, where she loves to hike and watch the deer devour her hosta.

Behind the Lies is her third novel published by She Writes Press. Her debut novel, *A Better Next*, was published in May of 2019, and *Finding Grace* followed in July of 2022.

Learn more at Maren's website,
www.marencooper.com.

SELECTED TITLES FROM
SHE WRITES PRESS

She Writes Press is an independent publishing
company founded to serve women writers everywhere.
Visit us at www.shewritespress.com.

Finding Grace by Maren Cooper. $16.95, 978-1-64742-385-8. When Caroline, a gifted ornithologist who wants a life of travel and adventure, gets pregnant against her wishes, her husband, Chuck, assumes she will change her mind. She doesn't—and as their daughter, Grace, grows up, she falls through the devastating schism that grows between them.

A Better Next by Maren Cooper. $16.95, 978-1-63152-493-6. At the top of her career, twenty plus years married, and with one child left to launch, Jess Lawson is blindsided by her husband's decision to move across the country without her—news that shakes her personal and professional life and forces her to make surprising new choices moving forward.

Jenna Takes the Fall by A. R. Taylor. $16.95, 978-1-63152-793-7. When Jenna McGrath has the misfortune of becoming notorious at age twenty-four, she very quickly experiences the deluge of public shaming so prevalent in the modern age.

Appearances by Sondra Helene. $16.95, 978-1-63152-499-8. Samantha, the wife of a successful Boston businessman, loves both her husband and her sister—but the two of them have fought a cold war for years. When her sister is diagnosed with lung cancer, Samantha's family and marriage are tipped into crisis.

A Dream to Die For by Susan Z. Ritz. $16.95, 978-1-63152-557-5. When a therapist is murdered, records of his clients' dreams are stolen, along with his computer—and suspicion falls on Celeste Fortune, a rebellious member of his cult. To clear her name, Celeste and her friend Gloria set out to find the real culprit, but as they discover the power of the stolen dreams, they become the killer's next targets.

Del Rio by Jane Rosenthal. $16.95, 978-1-64742-055-0. District Attorney Callie McCall is on a mission to solve the murder of a migrant teen, but what is she to do when her search for the killer leads her straight to the most powerful family in town—her own?

The Happiness Thief by Nicole Bokat. $16.95, 978-1-64742-057-4. Happiness is relative. For single mother Natalie Greene, that relative is her stepsister, Isabel Walker, known as The Happiness Guru. But even with Isabel's guidance, Natalie can't control her recently re-triggered PTSD over her mother's death in a car crash years ago. The old dread. The nightmares. And that all-consuming, terrifying thought: *I think I killed my mother.*